PACO IGNACIO TAIBO II

JUST PASSING THROUGH

PACO IGNACIO TAIBO II

JUST PASSING THROUGH

TRANSLATED BY

Martin Michael Roberts

CINCO PUNTOS PRESS

EL PASO, TEXAS

Originally published in Mexico in 1986 as *De Paso* by Leega Literaria.

Just Passing Through. Copyright © 1986 by Paco Ignacio Taibo II. Translation copyright © 2000 by Cinco Puntos Press.

FIRST EDITION

10 9 8 7 6 5 4 3 2 1

Library of Congress Cataloging-in-Publication Data

Taibo, Paco Ignacio, 1949-
   [De paso. English]
   Just passing through / by Paco Ignacio Taibo ; translated by Martin Michael Roberts. — 1st. ed.
       p. cm.
   ISBN 0-938317-47-4 (hc : alk. paper)
   I. Roberts, Martin Michael.   II. Title.
PQ7298.3.A58D413   2000
863—dc21

                                                    99-33494
                                                    CIP

NATIONAL ENDOWMENT FOR THE ARTS

This book is funded in part by generous support from the National Endowment for the Arts. Cover illustration taken from Diego Rivera's "Día de muertos." Copyright © the estate of Diego Rivera. Reproduction authorized by the Instituto Nacional de Bellas Artes y Literatura de México, and by the Banco de México, fiduciary in the Fideicomiso relative to the Museums of Diego Rivera and Frida Kahlo.

COVER DESIGN BY VICKI TREGO HILL
Printed in Canada by Best Book /Transcontinental Printing Inc.

For Benito y Carlos
— *indispensables carnales* —

For Astor Piazzola with his accordion,
& Gerry Mulligan on baritone sax,
who—with "Years of Solitude"—
put two months of this saga to music

"Perhaps time has a different ring to it for you,
like a constant reminder from the past in the present,
whatever that may be."
—*Joel James*

"There is nothing better than being on board
when the shipwreck comes along."
—*Benito Taibo*

A NOTE FROM THE AUTHOR

Much of what is written on the pages that follow is faithfully based on original documents, like conference minutes, police files, reports from foreign secret agents, witnesses' memoirs, articles from union newspapers, magazines and national newspapers.

It would be difficult to describe this work as a novel.

ANOTHER NOTE FROM THE AUTHOR

The majority of what is written on these pages has been reconstructed using the author's imagination, as well as his personal and not very reliable accounts of events that took place in Tampico, Atlixco, Veracruz and Mexico City between 1920 and 1923. The documentary evidence is just the framework around which the fiction is built.

It would be difficult to describe this work as a documentary; it is obviously a novel.

A FINAL NOTE FROM THE AUTHOR

Just what the hell is a novel?

1

WIRE GREENE TO HOOVER. SICT 23011. REF 1023. SAN
ANTONIO. RETRANS NEW ORLEANS. REPT BRIEFING AUG
18, 1920.

NEWS SAN VICENTE INVOLVED INVEST PRES WILSON
ASSASSINATION ATTEMPT. SEEN N ORLEANS C JULY 16
LAST W JOSE RUBIO (REF 1027). BOTH CONNECTED
ANARCHISTS GROUP BASED TAMPA FLA. CUBAN-BORN
TOBACCO WORKERS. SPECIAL CONTACT MATEO VEGA,
VEGAS OR VIGAS (REF 1927/11). SAN VICENTE
PROBABLY LEFT COUNTRY, ATTEMPTING TO LEAVE,
TO LEAVE SOON. FILE REF IWW EAST COAST
ACTIVITIES. INVESTIGATION UNDER WAY. SAN
VICENTE SENTENCED TO DEPORTATION BUT FEDERAL
TRIAL PENDING RE ASSASSINATION ATTEMPT. DETAILS TO
FOLLOW.

    DOLLY.

WIRE HOOVER TO GREENE TO DOLLY. URGENT COPIES TO CHESTER AND WILCOX. WASHINGTON. BRIEFING REPT SICT 23118. REF 1023 AND 1027. AUG 20, 1920.

ALL PORTS ARREST WARRANT SAN VICENTE AKA RUBIO. PREVENT DEPARTURE FROM COUNTRY. FOLLOW UP IF THE CONTRARY. AUTHORIZATION LIMITED TO MEXICO, CUBA, CANADA. MAX ALLOCATION SIX AGENTS FOR SAME.
    HOOVER.

———

WIRE BAXTER TO DOLLY. RETRANS DOLLY TO HOOVER. SICT 24911. REF 1023 AND 1027. SEPT 2, 1920.

SAN VICENTE AKA RUBIO LOCATED. RUMORS LOCATED THEM IN N ORLEANS. FALSE TRAIL SET UP BY THEMSELVES. TRYING TO CROSS BORDER DEL RIO, TEX. AGENT FOLLOWING WITH COVER.
    BAXTER.

———

WIRE LYMAN TO HOOVER. SICT 25013. REF 1023 AND 1027. SEPT 6, 1920.

RUMORS IN ANARCHIST CIRCLES NEW YORK LOCATE RUBIO, SAN VICENTE HERE, ATTEMPTING LEAVE COUNTRY. CONFIRMATION IMPOSSIBLE, ALL PORTS WARNING.
    LYMAN.

WIRE DOLLY TO HOOVER. SAN ANTONIO RETRANS. SICT
25819. REF 1023. SEPT 7, 1920.

CALVERT WOUNDED IN FOOT BY SMUGGLERS, DEL RIO, TEX.
SAN VICENTE LEAD FALSE. INVESTIGATION HERE ABANDONED.
APOLOGIES.
      BAXTER.

═══════════

WIRE HOOVER TO GREENE. GENERAL BULLETIN. REF 1023
AND 1027. SICT 25910. SEPT 9, 1920.

RESULT NEW YORK INVESTIGATION PROVES SAN VICENTE
AKA RUBIO NOT INVOLVED WILSON CASE. STILL INTEREST TO
APPREHEND VIA DEPORTATION FROM CUBA, WHERE CASE
PENDING RE MURDER POLICE OFFICER HAVANA. MAINTAIN
PRIORITY. MAX POSSIBILITIES SOUTHEAST COAST.
      HOOVER.

═══════════

WIRE CHESTER TO DOLLY. NATURAL. REF 1023 AND 1027.
SEPT 12, 1920.

LYMAN FOUND IN BAY BY TUGBOAT. ASSERTS THROWN IN
SEA FROM GERMAN MERCHANT SHIP BY SAN VICENTE, WHOM
HE FOUND AMONG PASSENGERS. LYMAN SEVERE PNEUMONIA
CAUSED 11 HOURS IN WATER. SAN VICENTE SHIP CALLS
MEXICO, HAVANA, PANAMA. LYMANS STATE PRECLUDES
MORE DETAILS. BLAMES SAN VICENTE AT TIMES, HIS COUSIN
LEO BRUCE AT OTHERS. SUGGEST HANDLE INFO WITH CARE.
      CHESTER.

2

"But why Mexico?" I asked Sebastián San Vicente 65 years later.

"And why the bleedin' hell not?" *

"You won't find the revolution there, San Vicente. In 1920 the country was worn out with so much armed struggle, so many dead, so many broken promises. There wasn't even an anarcho-syndicalist movement, although the CGT was about to be formed in a few months."

"I don't need to find a revolution waiting for me. A revolution's something you have inside you, and you carry it around. It's like luggage."

"That sounds like a nursery rhyme."

"That's it. That's just what it is," he said with a smile, and he went off along the bridge on the Seawolf, covered by the fine foam thrown up from the waves that came crashing down on the deck. He disappeared—beginning our story.

I remained in my Mexico City home 65 years later, watching the starlight through the window. The only thing that bothered me was that in 1920 there were still 29 years left for me to be born.

Translator's Note: Since San Vicente is a Spaniard, I have him speak a British slang as opposed to the American slang of his comrades—this maintains a verbal contrast.

3

They told me that since I had turned sixteen that day, I was now a man. I didn't take any damned notice of them. I went down to the harbor to see people getting off the ships. All the way I knew I was going to the port and it didn't matter if I closed my eyes because I would never get lost. I could just follow my nose and the smell of rancid grease, garbage, sweat and greasy spoon joints. Even if I had had no sense of smell, I could have heard my way because the same sea breeze brought noises along with it—crane engines, crashing gears and the sad music from a cathouse called "El Tropical." There were a lot of things in the air that day because you do not get to turn sixteen very often, big inside your gray overalls and under the straw hat an old-timer gave you—because some other old-timer gave it to him when he was young. The breeze smelled of dollars, shiny bills with fresh green ink on them, of the sort I did not have. And the breeze smelled of oil, because it smells of oil everywhere in Tampico. And the breeze sounded like a romantic ballad.

As I remember those sounds, those smells, I think I knew I was going to the port to see ships I would not be sailing away on. Those smells make me think Tampico has changed, that it no longer smells of dollars. But I did not think that way then, I could not even begin to think that straw hats were much better than the ones they make nowadays.

But the smell was there that day, and I was there with it, and the smell of the sea breeze, of rancid grease, of oil and dollars came down from the palm trees, slithered down the white-walled houses and was a little bleached by the sun.

People were coming ashore from the Morro Castle—a pert little Ward Line steamer—and from the Seawolf, anchoring at Tampico on its way from New York to Veracruz and then Panama before going back via Havana and New Orleans. The gangplank was down, and at the bottom policemen sat at a folding table, skillfully (like magicians and conjurers) picking up bribes, a tribute to the god who is in charge here. The priests from the church of the great bagman in the sky looked at me suspiciously because they do not like outsiders disturbing the ritual of ripping foreigners off— it was a private deal between the foreigners and them, like between a whore and a client, with no voyeurs allowed. I smiled with a face that said *there's enough to go round*—which is also understood, and quickly, among gypsies—and made a sign like I was going to help carry heavy bags for small change if God willed it—and even if he did not, because I had little to do with God then, and nothing at all now.

But I was not down there to carry bags for nickels and dimes—you don't do that the day you turn sixteen. I went to see guys coming from other countries, to look at the women in their flowery dresses and parasols and, with a bit of luck, to see some German sailors' uniforms, or the white vest of some gringo hustler who had come to liven up the gaming houses that the Chinese had set up in Tampico in those days; or I had come to see a black guy because I had not seen any for a while, or probably a Cuban band that was going to play at the Hotel Inglés. I felt I was not there just to pick up tips.

I know that I did go there for tips really, but tips in the form of eyes, feelings, dreams, which is something I did back then and keep on doing years later. It was just that things didn't turn out that way, because the third guy who came ashore stared at me and said, "Can you be trusted?"

"No," I answered.

"Well, well," he said, and walked on.

I suppose I was won over because he didn't try to convince me, he didn't try to buy me off because he probably guessed I was already sixteen and wasn't asking permission to live...that and the white vest. I let him walk a dozen paces, and caught up with him. He was waiting for me. How did he know?

"Solidarity, my friend, solidarity is something you don't buy. I appealed to you and you replied, that's all," he told me a year later when we were beside another ship.

We looked at each other for a while. Then he asked me, "Can you take me to your comrades? Is there an anarchist organization in Tampico?"

"You going to go along dressed all fancy?"

"I haven't got any other clothes to my name, friend." And that was true. He had no more than the clothes he stood in, and a little kit bag with some ironware in it—like a pistol, I said to myself. I later found out the bag had a plain set of wrenches and other mechanic's tools.

I went off to walk around the streets without waiting

for him. I was sixteen and a guide, not a companion. The guy quickly followed my dancing feet. We turned at the bridge and went to the Workers of the World House. We all knew the House in Tampico, me included. Like many, I had learned to read in *El Pequeño Grande*, and I delivered newspapers for old Gudiño, or with the guys from the Local Federation. I knew the "Red Declaration of Independence" poem by heart, and recited it in festivals. I knew the anarchists' Marseillaise, and sometimes wrote manifestos for the carpenters (as long as they dictated them, of course). I was the son of Red and—oddly enough for those times—an unknown mother. Now I think it's more common to have an unknown father, but not in my case. I was Red's son. I never knew my mother and never asked. Red was so called for having red hair, rather than for being an anarchist, but I was getting a name for myself now.

"What's your name, lad?" the new arrival asked.

"I used to be Little Red Pablo."

"What do you mean 'used to be'?"

"Because now I'm sixteen and just plain Pablo."

"All right," he said and stared at me. Then he held out his hand, "Mine's Sebastián San Vicente, and I'll use it again here," he said. I shook his hand firmly and if I say now that there were sparks flying off it, it's because time has gone by and you don't want to forget those things, never, but they should make their mark on Memory Lane forever. Because Memory Lane gets full of crap as time goes by, and there's things that need to be pointed out so as not to get washed away.

That was the first time I shook the hand of the best friend I ever had. Tampico smelled of oil, it was sunny, the sun was shining, the smell of green dollars wafted on the breeze through the streets, and I had met Sebastián San Vicente.

There was nobody in the House so we sat on the sidewalk to wait. Two drunks sat down to keep us company and sang, "Lovely Tampico/tropical port/you're the pearl of all the land/and I'll remember you anywhere."

And they repeated the last line: "I'll remembeeeeeer you anywheeeeere!"

San Vicente was neat and tidy and a stickler for cleanliness. He washed his hands two, three, six, eight or ten times a day. He said it was to get rid of the grease and soot stains he got from his days as a ship's mechanic. That was one of the many odds-and-ends I gathered from time to time about his life.

Things changed when I met San Vicente. I used to work all over the place, picking up loose change here and there. I delivered clothes for laundries, hustled clients for a couple of whores from Veracruz who let me sleep on their porch during the summer. I used to help Cosme, a Spanish storekeeper, to "sweeten" bottles of Havana rum (two to one, and don't tell anybody—half real Havana rum, the other half a mixture of industrial alcohol and burnt cane sugar), so in winter I could sleep on the counter in his store—La Vencedora—to get away from the rats and read the newspaper before Cosme used it to wrap things up in. I also worked as a typesetter's assistant, moving the lead blocks to the laying-out table, filling in columns and printing by hand and sweeping the floor. Well, to get to the point, ever since Red had died in an accident in boilerhouse No. 3 two years before, I had lost my profession as a son and hadn't found a new one.

San Vicente gave me a new profession. He knew you cannot live like a man without a profession. He gave me two, to boot—mechanic and firebug, too. He was a skillful mechanic—he spoke to engines in their own language while he fixed them. He whispered things to them. I later found out that he quoted them bits and pieces from the work of Malatesta* and Bakunin* as he tuned and fiddled with and adjusted them until they were purring along in the required, perfect way so they ran without wearing down or going out of kilter. He taught me how to do that. And while he was talking about engines, when he wasn't talking to them, he told me about the history of mankind according to Reclús.* He went along telling me about feudal villages and tribes, kings and the emergence of capital. He told me about the Paris Commune as if he had been there, about Red Barcelona and the May 1 Chicago Haymarket Martyrs like Louis Ringg who blew his face off with an exploding ciga-rette before they could hang him, and Oscar Neebe who—

---

*Translator's note: Errico Malatesta (1853-1932), an Italian; Mikhail Bakunin (1814-1876), a Russian; and Élisée Reclus (1830-1905), a Frenchman, were all anarchist revolutionaries, theoreticians and writers who had a great influence on Spanish anarchists like Sebastián San Vicente. They believed in communal autonomy, and, likewise, they believed that power was rightfully exercised from "the bottom up" rather than in a hierarchical and centralized manner. They were, therefore, antithetically opposed to Marxian communism with its emphasis on centralized political control by the state.

when he found he was only sentenced to 15 years and wouldn't share his comrades' fate—shouted to the judge "Hang me with them!"

And accompanied by his voice, countries and people would parade by. And everything around me was rounded off by seeing it all through new eyes, which I had just realized were mine after all.

I had heard that kind of deep, throaty, theatrical voice before, the voice of rebellion. I had sold its newspapers, I had been to rallies, I had heard oil workers screaming at the barefaced injustice meted out by the English, Dutch and gringo companies. I had seen the misery in our slums. I had heard the voice all right, but I had never felt the call for rebellion like a slap in the face, the kind of idea that grows inside you and breaks out of your skin and whispers softly in your ear in the name of destiny.

He was not a good speaker. He did not do a good turn in public meetings, or stir up the workers who gathered in the Workers of the World House. That was not his style. But he had organized some workers from the Communist local before he had been in Tampico a month-and-a-half, and they were the toughest nuts to crack, the most skeptical, the most daring, the most hard-line, dyed-in-the-wool, anti-management guys. No more than a dozen, and all with a feverish glow in their eyes.

We went to live together in an abandoned house by the Pánuco River. We did some carpentry and slept on the floor, side-by-side, looking at the sky through the holes in the roof.

He came home with Greta one day. She was a German

hooker I had seen in the Imperial Rooms drinking with gringo foremen from the oil companies. She was refined, a far cry from the rabble, and she was always dressed in pastel shades of chiffon.

San Vicente brought her home and she smiled. She didn't speak more than a few words of Spanish, so they spoke to each other in French. I suppose she was telling him her life's story which, as far as my experience goes, is what hookers always do for the first two or three months they know you. He would speak to her about other things.

We took exercise together, ran along the beach, dodging the patches of crude oil that drifted onto the sand and stuck there. We cooked strictly in turn and we made fritters. I taught them two songs. She taught us one whose lyric I never understood (Is that the one I sometimes sing? Am I singing about an enchanted forest, a fair, or the Virgin Mary?) and he taught us another one, a Cuban ballad he learned in a place called Gijón.

Greta swung between liveliness, attacks of hysteria, and a deep melancholy that left us all in a bad mood. San Vicente and I sometimes went around the oilfields, working on the engines, talking to people, or taking endless walks along the coast.

San Vicente did not come home to sleep one day. Greta and I, after hanging around our little room for a bit, dropped onto the mattresses we replaced the floor with. I was scared of her because I had heard her moaning in the night while she was asleep, because I had heard the chiffon shuffling when San Vicente gently undressed her. I dragged my mattress out onto the balcony and tried to sleep there. She came along naked with the night, stroked my hair and lay down by my side. Her breasts were heaving. I closed my eyes and put my hand between her legs.

Her white skin glowed in the moonlight and there were tears in my eyes when we finished making love and we hugged each other as we perspired. I felt I had cheated on my friend, that I had taken something of his without asking permission—I had stolen from him. Then I fell asleep. San Vicente woke us up in the morning with the smell of freshly made coffee. I tried to hide and he just smiled at me. She asked him something. She was showing off her nakedness just like the night before, but it was cloudy today so there was no sun to make her skin glow. He answered her first in French, and then turned around and translated for me.

"In jail. I spent the night in jail. The police took us all in for a rally we had last night."

Two or three hours later, as I was dragging my feet in the sand, he came to look for me to go to work. We had to repair a boiler that supplied hot water and heated up a hotel.

"She's not a belonging, my friend. You are not a belonging. I don't have any belongings, I just have comrades. Take it easy," he said. That was all he said.

Some time after, Greta killed herself by drinking arsenic which she had patiently distilled from flypapers. She did it in a hotel room in town so as not to involve us, I suppose. I never knew why. If she left a note, it wasn't for me. San Vicente never mentioned it.

San Vicente left Tampico a month later. He was going to Mexico City to represent the Communist local in a conference the red workers were going to organize. I thought

I'd never see him again. I said good-bye to him in the harbor because he was going to Veracruz first to take the train to Mexico City. He wore his white suit and was carrying his toolbag. I stayed behind in the harbor, alone, just sixteen, and with two professions.

4

There are no photographs of San Vicente. Not a single one. I have the impression (where from?) that he was a bit stiff and standoffish. There is a drawing of him, published in *El Demócrata* (Mexico City, February 1921), which I have in my hands. His eyebrows are joined together, he has a hooknose, a threadbare suit and vest, and his hair combed back. He looks around forty years old. Wrong, because he was not more than thirty. You get the impression that...I haven't a damned clue what the impression could be. What bothers me about this newspaper clipping is that he doesn't look like a happy man, because of that outward rigidity which seems to come from inside. The answer might be to imagine him half smiling, with one of those smiles that gives the owner a two-edged joke (laughing at the world and himself at the same time, like a character from a somewhat absurd tragedy). He needs a moustache. That's it, he needs a mustachio.

5

During the train ride from Veracruz to Mexico City, the well-dressed big-nosed Spaniard who answered to the name of Sebastián San Vicente did not confine himself to watching how the landscapes on the plain gave way to mountains that were almost in the clouds. He did not just disappear between the trees that shook in the breeze from the passing train, nor did he just think about rearranging the meager information he had about Hernán Cortés' epic journey through Mexican lands (information that was, really, almost all mistaken—he didn't get anything right. Cortés did not doze off in that forest, nor did he climb these mountains, nor did he go down into that volcano there to get sulfur to make gunpowder). On top of all that—in a little notebook with just a few leaves—he jotted down notes about Tampico, wrote a few unfinished letters, and balanced some accounts... A pair of pickpockets who worked for Slippers stole the notebook from him in San Lázaro station, who in turn passed it on to a reserve policeman, who then turned it over to the authorities and, years later, it turned up on the desk of Gendarmerie Capt. Arturo Gómez.

The notebook, among other things, said the following:

• The region's main union will be an oil union, and will not be centered around Tampico or Villa Cecilia; it will start up in the oilfields and refineries like Mata Redonda, Chapopote de Núñez, Juan Casiano, Tres Hermanos, El Ébano, Cacalilao, Cerro Azul, Esperanza, La Laja, Campo Naranjos, the Aguila refinery, Potrero...

• Owed: to Gudiño, 2 pesos; to García, six and a half pesos; to Pantaleón, a vest; to Fernando, six .38 bullets; and to Rebeldía, one and a half pesos worth of newspapers.

• My dear friend: You were right, just two days and I'm surrounded by dreams. The last traces of the skin infection that plagued me last month have gone now. I probably wasn't eating right, and the food on board ship and what my friends in Veracruz gave me sorted me out. I delivered the package you gave me to comrade Miño, who was very grateful and promised to send you and your partner a box of mangoes, along with a box of lemons for you to give to Alonso, the one who works the printing press, as he says that breathing in so much lead can be bad for you, but that lemons are good for stopping that. It must be like the scurvy that sailors get when they don't eat enough fresh fruit and water for a while. I only sold 40 newspapers in Veracruz from the pile you gave me, 20 of them to Miño, 17 to comrade Herón Proal and three I gave away to some longshoremen. They promised to send the money directly to you and...

• "The god hypothesis is useless." Sebastián Faure.

• If a worker makes three thousand screws a day and the total cost of the raw materials is 600 pesos, and the wear and tear on machinery amounts to 6 pesos, and costs of installation, electricity, etc. come to 11 pesos, and the boss sells them for 1,300 pesos then...the boss is a right bastard.

6

The blond gringo with a face like a Jewish tailor is Martin Palley from the IWW. Just over there by his side is Proal, a Veracruz tailor, the one who chaired the workers' conference in '16. The one writing, then, is Valadés, a Communist student; the one who looks so serious next to him, with a suit and tie like an office worker, is Araoz de León, leader of the new phone workers' union... In the row behind, the one with the beard next to the woman is Leonardo Hernández, who led the millers' strike in '19. No, I don't recognize that one—right next to Quintero— yes—he's come to represent textile workers in Atlixco and Puebla. Then there's the municipal workers, and the soap-makers, and Durán from the Valley of Mexico Textile Federation, then there's a Spaniard, San Vicente, up from Tampico...

7

Hanna to Hurley (to Hoover). State Dept.,
Mexico City, April 18, 1921.

Consular Info. Dept gathered following
info from several sources at your
request. Mentions that appear in
parentheses marked J.A. correspond to
informant Col. Miller, military attaché
here. Those without source ref. originate
in press cuttings evaluated in consular
section. Those marked B.S. correspond to
agent Bockman, State Dept. consular
attaché.

San Vicente, Sebastián

Born Spain, Gijón, port in north of
country, or in Guernica (BS) near Bilbao.
Son of well-to-do family (JA), left home
due to adventurous spirit. Aged 25-28
years. Has been naval machinist, boiler
mechanic (JA). Been to many ports as
sailor or naval mechanic. In USA, been

to N.Y. several times, after sailing
along East Coast. While there, one of the
most active members of anarchist groups
and IWW. Said to have been involved in
Mayflower assassination attempt when Pres.
Wilson got back Europe (JA). Escaped while
suspects were rounded up, stowed away on
ship bound for Cuba. When thought to be
in US, was in Cuba, Santiago province,
where implicated in sabotage attacks on
US merchant ships during sailors' strike.
Actions unknown on return to US.
Reported to be in Tampico end 1920, then
Mexico City as delegate from Red Brothers'
Group. Lodged in bakers' union local
during congress and days following. Not
known to have regular work. Known
practicing anarchist. Future plans unknown.
Distinguishing marks: three-inch scar
left armpit (BS). Good shot. Wins prizes
in fairs. Heard to say will return to US
soon to settle unspecified unfinished
business.

8

"Can you type, San Vicente?"

"With two fingers."

"That all?"

"But very fast, and with no spelling mistakes."

"Good. I then propose that comrade San Vicente be the correspondence secretary," Quintero said with relish.

San Vicente looked at him through half-closed eyes. He had not found that very funny.

"Those in favor?...five. Against?...one—San Vicente himself."

It was not that he thought lightly of the matter. In an organization that stretched across a country that was enormous to him, with no money to pay expenses for those that traveled, with no paid leave from factories, correspondence was the only thing to build up the organization, to make it nationwide. But still, battering the Remington with two fingers night after night seemed a small, barely useful task to him. He said to himself, *Patience is work, too.* And that month he began to recognize Carmona's scribbling, from Chihuahua, Castellanos' flowery letters from Mexicali, snatches of poetry by Aurelia Rodríguez from Cárdenas in San Luis Potosí, and Bruschetta's neat writing from Puebla.

He began to see his correspondents' faces, and imagine the rooms where they wrote by the light of an oil lamp. What should have been his secretarial notes—duly terse minutes strictly in keeping with assembly resolutions, telegraphic debates on how to see the world—began to go haywire. He began to put personal touches to them. He began a correspondence with Carmona in which, little by little, the main issue became Faure's thesis about the non-existence of God. He forced Castellanos to study political economics to debate by mail the fairness of employees' wages in a libertarian world. He almost drove Bruschetta mad involving him in an argument on birth control (the most modern methods, Malthus' theory, the geometric progression in population growth, the fertility span for women), and the man was an out-and-out homosexual. He got wound up in an almost incomprehensible argument by mail with Aurelia Rodríguez over the rules governing sonnets.

Within two months, you could say what you liked about the efficiency of the Confederation's correspondence secretary, but not that he didn't have a sackful of mail to answer every week.

9

"Get down to Atlixco. That's where you can be useful, that's where you'll find a task suited to your talents."

"And just what are my talents?" said San Vicente.

It was raining, just like it does in Mexico City, and the two men were huddled under the porch of a theatre opposite the Café Imperial since they had no money to go in for coffee with biscuits, which were in fashion then. San Vicente raised his eyes to the clouds to see water slicing through the air before crashing down into puddles. It was not like Gijón, where the rain was almost invisible—here you felt the rain hit your clothes and smack you in the face. But not back there, where it soaked you almost by accident.

"A mission for somebody like yourself, somebody who isn't scared of death."

"Who isn't scared of death?"

How far it all seemed from that damp room from which he used to see the streetlamp and the sea and the beach just beyond it.

"Is Atlixco by the sea?" he asked.

"No. It's in Puebla state, up in the mountains. A long way from the sea, my friend."

"All right." The sea would not have that dark green color

anyway, nor would it be as rough as in Cantabria. It would be a soft, pliant sea like in the Gulf of Mexico, that got bad-tempered and awkward every now and again.

"Will you accept? We could give you food and board as long as you're with us."

"And what would I have to do?"

"The textile federation belongs to the organization. We've got half-a-dozen big unions up there, places with 5,000 workers, like the Volcán mill, or at Metepec. But there's no propaganda, no newspaper, no working on ideas, no lectures. Worse still, the bosses are always hassling the Confederation. They send their gunslingers in, they get the army to break up strikes, they stop us from collecting union dues. There's a lot of work to be done up there."

"And does it rain in Atlixco like it does here?"

"Sometimes less, sometimes more," the man said, without really knowing what San Vicente would have preferred.

10

Puebla City, Puebla
March 11, 1921

Dear Slim,

I took my time to write you, but I'm
sure you can imagine why. We haven't had
a minute to think since the congress,
let alone to put pen to paper. It's all
to do with a campaign to get the workers
organized, which we hope will get
through to the textile groups in Mexico
City that are infested by scabs from the
CROM.*

We got the first issue of El Trabajador,
and it has circulated well, although
economically it was a flop, as ever. I
suppose that's due to our lack of

Translator's note: The Regional Confederation of Mexican Workers
(CROM) is a labor union confederation set up in 1918, with very
strong ties to generals Obregón and Calles, whose faction took control of Mexico after the revolution. It retains very strong links with
the government to this day.

experience in financial asset management. We'd make lousy capitalists. Even so, I'll send you a money order for 12 pesos and forty cents. Could you give Roberto the enclosed list of Confederation stamps I need for the new Atlixco chapters?

San Vicente's up there in Atlixco, and really active to boot. Our comrade has been a real boost to the Confederation here, above all since he's not tempted by the provocations of the bosses or the scabs. I've asked him to write you a piece for the newspaper, and he promised to do so as soon as he could. I said I hoped we wouldn't have to wait until he was laid up in the hospital with gunshot wounds. He answered nonchalantly (you know what he's like) that he hoped he'd catch a slug in his left arm so he could write you just what you want. He asks you to pass the word on to the committee that he'll resume his post just as soon as he can and things have cleared up.

Bye for now, brother.

Yours in anarchy,

Antonio Bruschetta

11

The boss at the Cantabria mill said to me:

"Hey, Tomás, you want a thousand pesos?"

I said yes, and asked him, "Who do I have to kill?"

"That damned Spanish anarchist, San Vicente."

"Fifty-fifty," I told him, and he understood straight off, as he's a wise-ass for business.

"Three hundred up front, and the rest when the pictures of his corpse come out in the newspapers."

"And if there's no picture?"

"The news will do," he said, spreading the money out on the table like it was a deck of cards. The son of a bitch was giving me all one and five peso bills so they'd seem a lot, and they did. I picked up the stack of money and bowed out, touching my hat with two fingers.

I went to the cantina to think things over and I thought, If I go to the Guadalupana, the owner there'll probably give me another three hundred; if I talk to the scabs in Puebla, they'll likely give me two hundred for the lot; if I talk to the Archbishop, I'll get an indulgence in advance; if I sell the story to *El Universal*, I might get another three hundred. Because I kill for money, I ain't no jerk, and I'm out to set up a tannery some day in Juárez or Jiménez, a long ways from here, anyway.

That's where I was when San Vicente came in. I made like I was getting over woman trouble with a few drinks, but he came right up to the table and sat down in front of me.

"I'm told you were given some bills to kill me," he said straight off and without so much as a hello.

I had my hand in my jacket pocket, and I had...I just had to have...my finger on the trigger and the automatic cocked and ready. So I came right out with it and nodded.

"How much?"

"Three hundred," I told him. And I wondered who the snitch had been; the word was out before they'd even finished counting out the money.

"Take the money out of your vest pocket with your two fingers and put it on the table," he told me. People were gathering round, and they were no assholes either, all getting behind him. It was clear that if there was going to be a shoot-out, it would all come my way.

I spread the money out like a deck of cards, just like they'd given it to me.

"You know this isn't for me. I won't touch a penny of it."

I nodded again, then it dawned on me.

"Thanks," he said, and got up. "You do know who squealed and why?" he asked me before he went out.

"I think I already got that one figured."

San Vicente went out of the cantina without even looking round. I drank my half-finished tequila and walked slowly out.

That asshole of a boss at the Cantabria squealed to some working stiff there so if I didn't kill San Vicente, he'd kill me, and then he'd send the cops in to finish things off. It wasn't the double-cross that bothered me most, it was the lack of trust.

So I went along to the Cantabria offices and put a slug between the wise-ass's eyes. His blood got all mixed up with his spit on the mahogany desk. Stiffs do some weird things.

So that's how I come to be up by the border, buying and selling stiffs, instead of having a tannery.

12

There are not any streets around named after him. Even now he is just a blot, a piece of mist. "The Shadow of the Shadow," I am going to call him and some other friends in a future novel.

Looking through files, old papers and microfiche, the name crops up here and there. Sometimes enough to string a bit of a story together, but never enough to finish it off. There is not a single piece with his byline on it, no conference speech taken down in shorthand, or even a whole article. There are no photos, no rent receipts in his name (he never had a home), no wedding certificates or birth certificates for his children. Just bits and pieces in the press that add up to a trace of the man.

Once when I was in Washington, D.C., in the basement of the National Archives, I did a computer search to turn over the FBI's database for all the information they had on lists of foreign anarchists who had roamed around Mexico. I waited in the white-walled booth in which I was closed up. The computer rejected the name Sebastián San Vicente. I suppose that is where this story was born.

I wrote his name again, joining up the two words in his surname (Sanvicente), and the computer grudgingly gave me a list of files, that half an hour later turned into six rolls of microfilm, which a girl with spectacles like bottle tops brought to my electronic cavern. There was San Vicente's escape from the United States, and the classified reports on him sent up from Mexico now and again.

Why do I chase shadows?

Is it so I can talk to them?

13

He was a strange man, who thought that poverty was ennobling, that everything was shared when you had nothing—and he lived that way, or almost. Atlixco allowed him to plunge right into poverty. Not the poverty of appearances you saw in the slums he had known in Havana or New Orleans, not the dignified and patched-up poverty you saw in Pueblo Nuevo, the Barcelona neighborhood. No, this was raw straightforward poverty. In Zenón's house, where they put him up, he shared a bed with two boys aged nine and eleven, and a girl of six. When he chose to sleep on the floor, Zenón was offended. They had invited him there because it was one of the few houses that had a bed. Zenón himself slept with his wife on a straw mat in a little room (the kitchen). Javier, his eleven-year-old bedfellow, worked twelve-hour shifts in Metepec, just like his father, because they were piece-workers. They ate just twice a day at home, at breakfast and suppertime. When they had meat, just once a month, there was not enough to go around. Zenón only had one pair of pants. San Vicente had two, so he gave a pair to Javier.

14

Dear Pancho,

  San Vicente asks me to tell you he will be ready to write for <u>El Trabajador</u> around the end of June. He went through Puebla like a black wind, spreading ideas--some hare-brained, some less so-- and I have come by reports about him on his arrival at Atlixco. They tell me he has been very active in our textile federation locals (Pacheco, who passed through on his way back to Veracruz, will fill you in; there are things I do not like to trust to the mail) and among the hands on the local plantations. He went tooth and nail at the authorities in Atlixco, and managed to spring Sandoval from jail. Sandoval had been framed for robbery by the boss at Metepec and his cronies. Something good must come of all this because, just as I told you in another letter and as Marqués will have told you, things are unbearable in Atlixco. We shall talk of this some other time. Regarding the Bakunin leaflets you sent me, I must point out there were 98 of them, not a hundred, of which I have sold 67 and I will wire you the money today. I can well understand the hardship the organization is suffering and that it cannot be bankrolling cowpokes in the boondocks like me. By the way, I will be getting hitched to a comrade from hereabouts next June, whom you have not had the pleasure of meeting...

15

FROM CAPTAIN BARCENA TO MILITARY HQ PUEBLA REGION.
ATTN MAJOR R. V. SALAZAR DUARTE.

AGITATION AMONG PEASANTS CONFIRMED IN SAN DIEGO,
LA BLANCA, ESTRELLA AND OTHER PLANTATIONS. GROUP
CGT ACTIVISTS LED BY SEBASTIÁN SAN VICENTE ENGAGED IN
VIOLENT CONFRONTATION WITH HANDS AND FOREMEN
METEPEC WORKS. YESTERDAY THEY TOOK BOSSES
CONFEDERATION OFFICES WITH SHOUTS OF VIVA FATHER
HIDALGO* VIVA LENIN LETS KILL THE SPANISH BASTARDS.
ABSURD THING WHOLE STORY SAN VICENTE LEADING THEM
IS OBVIOUSLY SPANISH AS ALL WHO KNOW HIM TALK OF HIS
STRONG ACCENT. REQUEST INSTRUCTIONS ON MATTER.
     BARCENA

Translator's note: Father Hildago—known as the father of his country—was born in 1753. On September 16, 1810, from his pulpit in Dolores, Guanajuato, he gave el Grito ("the shout")—Mexico's declaration of independence from Spain. He was executed by a firing squad on July 30, 1811.

16

Yes sir, they were chanting "Viva la Virgin of Guadalupe! Viva the soviets! (or the sovierts, I'm not sure how you spell those chants), Viva Lenin! Viva anarquía!" Nobody told me, I heard it all with these pointed ears my own whoring mother gave me.

They jumped over the walls and fences with machetes in their hands, waving the hats as they had no flags and hollering, singing songs, each one their own.

They took three plantations the same day, being real sure they belonged to the same ones who owned the factories. There were no dead, just two or three foremen beaten up.

I saw something unusual in San Diego. They dragged a load of furniture out into the yard to make room for the squatters to sleep indoors. They had dragged the furniture out carefully, like they were the new owners who wanted to take real good care of it, and covered it with dustsheets. There was even a grand piano there which looked like it had never been used—because the owner's daughters were more interested in the foremen than culture—so the piano really stood out.

Then San Vicente shows up. I knew him because I'd seen him at a rally in Atlixco. Well, damn me if he doesn't just sit down and start playing Chopin's "Polonaises." The squatting workers gathered round and sat down on the ground, in the archways, or in the armchairs to enjoy the music. A little French-style fountain was pouring out water in time with the music, just like another instrument. If my musical training doesn't escape me, San Vicente was no maestro when he played. At times he cheated, skipping chords he couldn't remember too well, but he played them all with manic concentration, like a personal offering to Persephone, with a care and feeling that touched the audience. Chopin has always had the virtue of jerking a few tears from me, and that Chopinesque soviet was no exception, on that sultry afternoon on a plantation taken over by followers of Lenin, Bakunin, music and the Virgin of Guadalupe.

17

Those heavy clouds with rain written all over them and looming over the cobbled streets of Atlixco are not your clouds, I reckon. You think property is theft, even as far as clouds are concerned, and that nobody can take possession of country scenes, that they are here one day, gone the next. I am right with you there, that nobody can take possession of country scenes with impunity, that there is a price to be paid. You see them like a background, like patterns daubed on a white cloth you look at from over four yards back, so the brushwork fades from view and reveals a castle, the bridge of a ship or the Piazza San Marco. You think there is nothing hidden in that swollen drop of rain, that it just wets that black hat a little, the one a fallen comrade's widow gave you, and still reminds you of old times even if it no longer has the band that once ran around it. You see yourself as just a passerby. I see you as a black bird, an anarchic crow threatening to blow up with unleashed passion. I'm waxing lyrical at your expense. You take a walk through the cobbled streets of Atlixco and down mine.

18

A handwritten note at the top:
For encoding and retrans. to Col. Garvey, U.S. Military Intelligence, Washington. Miller.

In response to your expressed interest in Sebastián San Vicente and Richard F. Phillips, who goes by the name of Frank Seaman in Mexico. The former played no part in the railroad workers' strike, since he was in Atlixco, and only recently moved back to the General Worker's Confederation headquarters, where he is a secretary. As a pure anarchist, he has serious differences with Phillips, a confessed Marxist who was active in the railroad movement, speaking at rallies and promoting activism in minority groups in the CSF, as well as in the Communist press. Phillips lives with a Polish subject named Natasha Michaelowa, said to be a translator of Polish, Russian, French and English with the Communist International and to know Trotsky personally. She recently arrived in Mexico on board the

Hollsatia at Veracruz. I ate with them recently and, given my position in the Party, they told me how mail gets to Moscow via a group of German sailors who often come to Veracruz and Campeche on German and Norwegian ships. They also told me about the forthcoming arrival here of two Communist International delegates, one a Japanese called Sen Katayama, the other an American whose name they did not mention to me, but who will travel under the cover of an Austrian who distributes movies to Mexican theaters. Phillips was born some place in California and must have a file open with the U.S. authorities for draftdodging. He lives very modestly in López Street in a two-room house, but is not known to do any paid work, as he receives no pay whatsoever for the writing and translating work he does for the Party.

San Vicente, who appears with me in the enclosed photograph (Pablo Rosas, from the Ericson Telephone Company work-shops, is on my right, San Vicente, in the brown suit and spotted tie, is on my left), came back very excited from Atlixco. The committee sent for him because they felt more activity was needed in Mexico City after the railroad strike. It would give a last shove to knock over the scab unions, which were really hurting after their leadership sold out during the strike. His first appearance at the local caused some fun and games since he refused to discuss union problems, saying the place was a pigsty, and just picked up a broom and dustpan and cleaned the place up. He spent two days cleaning up, refusing to discuss anything or do any union work at all until he had finished. Rubio, Carmen Farías and de Quintero stared in astonishment while San Vicente, like any old washerwoman, just kneeled on the floor and polished the filthy wood-block floors--which really needed it. When he had finished, he said, "Now we can get to work," and warned them, "but mind you don't dirty the local, because if anyone does, I'll make him clean it up personally." Quintero, who always flicks his cigarette ash all over the floor now takes great care to tap his cigarettes on a saucer in his hand.

They say San Vicente and Phillips will organize a Labor Day rally in Morelia, and have several other propaganda rallies ready for that month. San Vicente, meanwhile, is working with garbage collectors and washerwomen, trying to organize them into unions. I tried to make conversation with him, but he avoids all personal information and sticks to ideas. He did not want to say anything about his time in Cuba or the US, although he spoke to me at length

about Hamburg and Shanghai, places he
is supposed to have been to a few times
as a sailor. He is a marine boiler
mechanic by trade. He works now and
again, fixing some boilers or cars for
a big company, just enough to get by.
He scratches enough to live a couple of
weeks or a month, because the work is
well-paid and he gets it over and done
with in two or three days, and that's
that. He sleeps wherever the night
finds him. He has a deal going that I
do not quite understand with a Chinese
laundry where they wash and press his
only suit, and he hangs around there.
What makes him even more dangerous is
that he is irreproachable, and people
like him, even if he gets very irritable
and violent at times. Both Phillips and
he believe the revolutionary movement
will get very strong among the workers
this year and next. I do not agree. The
masses are fed up and only stir occa-
sionally. What is more, the failure of
the rail strike has shattered a lot of
dreams. I will carry on reporting.

Allen

19

Mexico City
May 1921

The revolution will, I hope, bring a new
direction and pace to our western way of
life. I would like to see calmer, less
ambitious, slower, more patient, nature-
loving people arise. The skyscrapers
must be preserved as they are monuments
too, after all. There are no skyscrapers
in Mexico City, and people move slowly
along the street, and there is always
the gentle smell of flowers in the air.
We have more time to get to know each
other. Food is plainer, houses plainer
and prettier, the people--apart from
flashes of childish violence--are sunny,
sweet and unconsciously comradely. In the
United States radical movement, I found a
lot of socialists, but few comrades. You
just don't have time because even your
soul is indelibly tainted by the feverish
pace and the superficial impatience of
American society. There is something

different here, and even if I have yet to think it through, I know it is closer to the fraternity the new world must be built on.

It does not bother me. I just lie back and enjoy it. I don't know how to put it in words. My friend San Vicente, a disgraceful Spanish anarchist, tells me that it has to do with my having entered a society with nothing to lose, which I should understand full well as a Marxist. They've had so many broken dreams and have been plunged so quickly into the twentieth century that everybody takes things pretty much as they come. That's one way of looking at it. The other way that grabs us all is that comradeship is a higher form of friendship, and there is nothing better in this world than friendship.

I think he is wrong. I feel that here, they've been so close to death and lived so hand-in-glove with violence that life as something to preserve inside you has little meaning, which is why you have to give a bit more, and enrich it to make it worthwhile.

My impressions don't sound very Marxist, but I'm barely at the stage where I am learning to combine objective analysis, studying the heart of the system, its steel framework and its productive relationships, with subjective images and impressions.

I haven't had too much time to read
and study these last three weeks. The
pace of daily action has turned very
brisk with us being constantly on call
to talk at an assembly, take part in a
strike, talk at a rally, go out to this
or that meeting. It is a curious
contradiction; you have this slow-moving
country where everybody takes their
time then, suddenly, this great awakening of unionism and feverish activity
this last month-and-a-half. Everything
comes in spurts, in waves of activity. I
suppose that we'll get back to more
patient and careful work which will
have more to do with propaganda and
organization after the Labor Day rallies, which will finish about May 8, and
then I'll get back to studying and
writing poetry. San Vicente, the comrade
I've been telling you about, won't let
me think along these lines, telling me
that the pace will speed up over the
next two years, that we're seeing a
growing awakening among the workers and
their drifting back to the organization.
I rather think he believes what he likes.

Regards,

Richard Francis Phillips

20

Mexico City
May 14, 1921

From: The Presidency
To: The Interior and Foreign Affairs
Ministries

Issue arrest and deportation warrants
under the provisos of Article 33 of the
Constitution for the following foreign
agitators involved in the Morelos affair
and Chamber of Deputies incident:

Sebastián San Vicente, Spanish
Richard Francis Phillips, U.S.
Natasha Michaelowa, Polish
José Rubio, Spanish
Karl Limon, German
Sánchez, Colombian
José Allen, U.S.
J. Palley, U.S.
William Foertmeyer, U.S.

Please proceed forthwith.

F. Torreblanca, Secretary
by disposition of President A. Obregón

21

Maybe shadows have a certain density about them, but as for shadows of shadows—those elusive, misty and faint traces I find here and there—there is very little of the human warmth left that brought them about. Just scraps of news picked up from his friends over the years, mere scraps of scraps of scraps. Faint shadows.

Armando Bartra once told me that he took a liking to Mao Tse-Tung because one of his photos had a kind of ridiculous charm to it and made him seem human.

I cannot imagine San Vicente smiling. It seems as though I could easily lose him in an enormous station full of people.

22

Just as they were smashing the door down with rifle butts, Phillips was saying to San Vicente:

"The revolution is science, brother. As long as you don't understand that simple idea, you won't be able to put yourself in the right place, the right course, the...how d'you put it?...along the right track, the stream of history. History, that's it."

There were discussing this over a bottle of extra dry Havana rum placed on a small table between them. It was rather odd, as San Vicente was a teetotaler, and Phillips did not drink much. The Havana rum's role in this conversation was more decorative really, a stage prop rather than having any functional purpose. So, when the door was smashed into splinters thanks to the gendarmes' rifle butts, and one of the policemen ran in and hit the table with his gun-barrel, smashing the bottle in the process, it was no big deal. Phillips went to jump out of the window, but found two Mausers aimed at him from the floor below, just waiting for him to execute one last fatal pirouette in the air. He went back into the room and smiled at the police captain in charge of the operation.

"Come on, you gringo bum. Tell your friend to get out of the room."

San Vicente had gone into the bedroom and barricaded himself behind the double mattress and a dressing table.

"Come on out of there, San Vicente. They've got the place surrounded, and they've got rifles."

"And throw your gun in front of you before you come out," the captain shouted.

San Vicente's forty-five rolled along the waxed floor, and then followed the man, with his hands in the air.

"You're completely wrong, Phillips," he said, looking at his friend, without even glancing at the gun-barrels aiming at him. "The revolution is an act of will. What the bleedin' hell has science got to do with it?"

"Move your ass, jerk," a gendarme said, poking him with his rifle.

Phillips folded both his hands behind his head after putting on a leather jacket whose pockets had been searched by the captain. He began to walk toward the door.

"Will, will! All crap, if there's no sense of history. Will without class consciousness—bah!" he said, almost as a farewell. The rum bottle had rolled around the floor, and a policeman sucked out the last dregs and dumped it before leaving the room.

The discussion was interrupted as they left the house because the gendarmes threw San Vicente and Phillips into two separate cars, which took off down the back street towards the headquarters of the gendarmes on Mesones Street.

Phillips managed to bum a cigarette off them, and undid half of it to smoke in his pipe. San Vicente listened nonchalantly with his hands in his pockets as the deportation warrant was read out to him.

"You got anything to say, gentlemen?" the officer who was slumped in a leather chair asked.

"Where're we going to be deported to?"

"Since you both came across our northern border, that's where you'll be dropped off. Could be Reynosa or Matamoros, maybe Ciudad Juárez."

Phillips and San Vicente exchanged glances.

"Couldn't it be Guatemala?" the Spaniard asked.

"Wouldn't you prefer Cuba?" the gendarme asked.

"Major, you know we had nothing to do with what we're accused of, but I don't want to argue about that. You know, and I know, and that's that. But if we're deported to the U.S., they'll throw us in jail there. The same goes for San Vicente if he's sent to Havana..."

"I'm sorry, but that decision is out of my hands."

They spent the night on a bench outside the police officer's workroom.

"The main problem as I see it, getting down to brass tacks, has to do with this dictatorship of the proletariat business."

"That's just a passing phase, my friend. What else can you come up with in a revolutionary crisis? The only thing you can do is set up a dictatorship against the class enemy, disarm them, stop their attempts to retake power, subdue them, stop them sabotaging workers' organizations, dispossess them of all property and technical advantages. At the same time, you have to stop things getting out of hand with the more backward sectors in the proletariat. It's just a type of transition, a temporary dictatorship of the proletariat."

"I can see a lot of 'buts' in that. It's neither temporary

nor to do with the proletariat. It tends to be eternal, and it's a dictatorship by the Party, your party."

"But the Party represents the best of the class," said Phillips.

"That remains to be seen," San Vicente answered, and lay down on his half of the bench.

They were taken to the Carretero penitentiary, handcuffed, with chains around their ankles and a double guard. The sun bothered San Vicente during the escort, which was by foot, so they gave him a straw hat, since his Stetson had been lost during the raid. They walked slowly on a day when the wind blew up the dust along the way.

"But won't you agree with me that the working class cannot take power without organization?" Phillips asked.

"It needs to be unionized and broad-based," San Vicente answered, screwing his face up to try to stop the loose dirt getting into his eyes.

"What about the soviets?"

"Why not the soviets? But they must be soviets for all tendencies, soviets with room for all political organizations. Soviets elected from the grass roots, from the workers' assemblies."

"That's the way the soviets are in Russia."

"If that's the way they really were. But they've shut out the anarchists and social revolutionaries."

"They weren't elected in the last congress."

"They're being persecuted."

"They've acted against the revolution."

"They've acted against the Bolshevik dictatorship," said San Vicente.

"You guys'll never learn to accept the majority," Phillips answered as he limped along.

They slept on the floor in Carretero, without even a mat woven from corn shucks to sleep on. The stone slabs were damp, and Phillips began to cough in the night. He stood up. You could see the night through a window six feet up the wall. There wasn't a single star out. He lit his pipe, and it went out right away. The tobacco left in the pipe-bowl was burned out. He turned it over, but to no avail.

"The revolution can only prevail with centralization."

"A free federation of communities and branches of industry. Coordination, yes, but no centralization. Centralization just takes the initiative away from the producers," San Vicente said, seemingly asleep.

In the morning, another escort took them to the Colonia railroad station.

Phillips tried to sound out the officer in charge of the escort.

"Are we being sent north, south, to the Atlantic or the Pacific?"

"My orders are to take you to Manzanillo."

"Where the bleedin' hell's Manzanillo?" San Vicente asked.

"It's a port on the Pacific. From there they can send us by steamer to California, or to Peru."

"Or even China, for that matter."

"Yes, you can get to China across that sea," the American said.

"China. That wouldn't be bad," the Spaniard said.

"Talking about China, what do think? In a nationalist revolution, is the answer a maximalist program or an anti-feudal alliance? How can you solve the problem with the peasant majority? Do you believe in class alliances?"

The discussion started up again six hours later on the train. They were handcuffed to wooden seats that hurt their backs and backsides, with Phillips smoking his pipe while the train cut through the mountains on the Sierra Madre Occidental. San Vicente took the initiative.

"If Marx says the aim of the revolution is to abolish the state, why do Marxists worry so much about strengthening it? Why is Marxism in favor of nationalization? Why do they say that a planned economy means centralization?"

"Because you cannot reach the goal without first going through the stages," Phillips said, whose backache was not conducive to metaphysics.

"And less so if you go backwards," San Vicente answered, as the wooded countryside brought out the worst in him.

"Backwards and on your knees..." he added five minutes later, but Phillips was asleep.

The prison in Manzanillo was not a serious affair, and it was very hot too so they were taken to a central patio, flanked only by white two-story walls, and left to walk around without any more information than a "be seeing you," and soup, almost all of it water, twice a day.

"Are you a Bakuninite, one of Malatesta's pure anarchists, like one of those Spanish anarcho-syndicalists from the CNT, or what?" Phillips asked, and then added, "I met Pestaña in Moscow last year."

"I haven't had the pleasure. I happen to be an anarcho-syndicalist, or hadn't you noticed all these months we've been seeing each other? I like chorizo sausage, but I'm a vegetarian like all the Spanish working class," said San Vicente, half jokingly but half seriously.

After a couple of days, the officer in charge of the deportation turned up with Natasha Michaelowa handcuffed by his side.

"You have company, gentlemen, and news, too."

While Natasha and Phillips hugged one another, San Vicente listened to the news.

"You're all bound for Guatemala, thanks to the lady here who intervened with the government, even at the cost of her being deported as well. Within three hours, you'll be on board a steamer that will take you to Sipacate in three days."

"And what's that?"

"A commercial port belonging to the United Fruit Company, or so they tell me."

Phillips spent his time with Natasha. San Vicente spent his taking long walks around the ship, gulping down the sea air, nervously watching out for sea gulls and looking for storms that never came on the horizon.

The debate was not resumed.

23

Guatemala City
July 7, 1921

Dear José,

Sorry for writing to you in English,
but I want to be very exact in what I
have to say, and I prefer English to
Spanish. The comrade bearing this letter
is to be trusted and has instructions to
deliver it to no one but yourself. We
have been fairly active here, thanks
mainly to San Vicente rather than my own
merits, as he is very capable in union
work. He has managed to get some
active units going that we helped the
Guatemalan Worker's League to set up,
and he has also helped along unions
for carpenters and bakers in this
city. Our new comrades will help us to
cross the border on foot at the end of
the month near Tabasco. From there we
will try to cut across the jungle and
get to Veracruz by sea, where we will

get in touch with the organization again.

I am writing so you can cover up for us by leaking information to the press throughout July about our supposed activities in Guatemala, which you found out about by mail. You can make up some letters dated in Guatemala City. You can talk about meetings in the Imperial Theater, the inauguration ceremony for the bakers' union, and that we are work-ing on a newspaper to be called <u>El Obrero</u>. We shall resume contact from Veracruz, if all goes well. I will need a safe house in Mexico City for Natasha and myself, and entrust you to find one by the beginning of August. Tell K, but nobody else.

Greetings. For the social revolution!

R.F.P.

24

He has slept in a different place every night since he got back from Guatemala. He does not choose, or follow any preconceived plan. He simply waits for the time to come and sleeps wherever the night finds him—in a union local, in a house where a meeting has been held, inside a streetcar in a depot, protected by guards who belong to the union, in a park, in a vaudeville theater—taking advantage of a strike among the stage-hands—or even in a circus in the animal pen. He sleeps on benches, mats, camp beds, straw, whorehouse beds. He shares his nights and nightmares with an old giraffe, a young whore, with a telegrapher's kids, with his telephone worker friend Moisés Gutiérrez, with Rodolfo Aguirre, or he sleeps rough with the striking Colmena workers.

He shares his starry nights and dawns. He uses the same clothes until they fall to bits, and then begs, borrows or steals some more. He works from time to time—rolling cigars with tobacco leaves his comrades bring him from Veracruz, doing odd jobs as a mechanic, boiler repairer, or garbage collector.

He owns nothing, he has nothing to lose. The paper he writes on is from borrowed old leaflets, where he composes on the reverse side, or on the torn-off edges of postcards and newspapers, or end cuts from the presses at *Humanidad*. Whereas he once had a gold-plated fountain pen, he now uses pencil stubs he picks up here and there. He reads other people's books over and over again. He picks them up one day, wherever he may be—a house, a union library, a table during a meeting. He drops them off somewhere else the day after—some other house, another room or union library, or another table during another meeting. He comes and goes, and comes back again. He seems to have a nose for where confrontations are going to arise, where the mounted police are going to charge, where the firemen are going to lie in wait to aim their hoses at the strikers. He also knows where assemblies and rallies are to be held, as well as editorial meetings for the dozens of anarchist newspapers printed in the city.

He floats, turns around, and turns up.

At times, he seems like a shadow. He's the same San Vicente as in 1921, but with new magic gifts, like being right in the middle of a bonfire.

Where does he spend his free time? Who does he make love to? When does he dream? Where do his dreams go to?

25

San Vicente was sitting six rows back in the assembly hall with Rodolfo Aguirre when he whispered to him straight off:

"'You say something is impossible when you don't really want it.'"

"Malatesta?"

"Aha," the Spaniard answered him.

"I know a few like that, too."

"Out with them."

"'The strongest man is the least isolated one,'" said Aguirre, who did a stretch in jail in 1919 with a book by Malatesta as his sole company.

"How does this sound? 'Let others do what we cannot do better ourselves.'"

"Good, that's good. How about this one? 'We must watch out for believing that lack of organization guarantees freedom. Everything indicates it just is not so.'"

"I've got a better one," San Vicente said, after thinking it over for a while. "'Let the masses toil as their hearts desire.'"

26

"Well, I think homesickness is good for making soup with," San Vicente said one day. It was his way of saying he did not give a shit. He also used to say, "Ideologies are good for making paella." Or, "I can make a good stew out of fear." Which is to say, he could make good food out of what others use to write short stories, poems or novels with.

"What do you make with love, then, San Vicente?" the poet Miguel Riera asked him.

"Me? What I can," he said, proudly.

They had been walking on the edge of the Condesa racetrack and the poet was contending that the city was beginning to go to ruin, that all those modern suburbs with pretentious names—like Roma Sur Expansion, Condesa Residences, Hippodrome Park—were just patches of blacktop covering the dirt. San Vicente had replied that he could not care less about all this provincial soft talk, and finished off with that stoney phrase about making soup out of his homesickness.

"Have you ever paused to think, Miguel, about the slight difference made by sewers and quinine?" he said, quite convinced.

"I mean, you like machines and smoke billowing from chimneys..."

"And outhouses for that matter. I like cars, too, and if you push me and don't tell any one, I like Thompson machine guns, with reloadable drums holding fifty .45-caliber rounds that weigh 11 pounds four-and-a-half ounces and are two-feet-six and five-eighths of an inch long."

"As far as I am aware, these ideas of yours are not really compatible with anarchy," Riera said.

They had stopped to let four horse-drawn carriages carrying rich children go past—on their way back from a pilgrimage or a rodeo, or something like that. They were not really looking at the children's fancy clothes, just the horses.

"I'm sorry, Miguel, but I'm got going to be much use as a character in one of your novels, not even one who just appears to make the plot thicken. I'm a man who just passes through. I'm here and I'm not here. At times I have the daftest explanations, even for important things."

27

The city nowadays is not what it was back then. The city back then was not what it is now. Seventy-five years have not gone by for nothing. That is not the problem. It is nothing to do with trying to find the 1923 Mexico City in today's monstrosity. Nor am I going to get caught up in nostalgia for things I never saw, things I can hardly imagine. It has all to do with a professional problem. Once you realize that that city is not this one, you are left with the problem of finding that city. Newspapers have etchings in them, they talk about streetcar lines, of open spaces with corn ripening in them with nothing but a narrow road cutting across with the odd Ford or Packard wheezing along. Newspapers can supply the décor, the scenery—two patches of wasteland here, a street there, a man selling birds carrying ten cages piled up on his back like a tall pillar, a colonial building, ten streetcars in a depot, two men on horseback halfway down the Paseo de la Reforma. It's not that. It's more, that's just the danger—the temptation in believing the city is not the same as its décor. It's me that needs the pulse, the heart of the city, that feeling in the air which the Sunday music just hides, those provincial smells the big city has yet to blot out. And so San Vicente moves around on a large stage set, a soulless city. And that is my problem, not his.

28

The undersigned, who was sent on a
mission to find out whether there was
any truth to the rumor that the so-
called Pedro Sánchez (a.k.a. the
Tampico Man) was really the dangerous
Spanish anarchist, Sebastián San
Vicente, already deported once from
Mexican territory as a subversive. Who
turned up in a CGT assembly hall on
Uruguay Street, already known to the
authorities, who without having met the
above-mentioned San Vicente and having
no more than a photograph to identify
him, referred to it to make a
comparison with the speaker at the
assembly of striking workers from the
Colmena and Barrón mills, and discovered
a remarkable likeness as well as noticing
that the Tampico Man actually spoke with
a Spanish accent--from Spain--rather
than what you would expect from the
northeastern Mexican port.

Unfortunately, the undersigned was

seen to take the photograph out of his
pocket, and was detained at the ending
of the meeting by textile workers and
forced to eat it. As this was the only
photograph this department had of the
above-mentioned San Vicente, we hereby
respectfully request...

29

I have always had an aversion to Holy Joes. There's a necessary amount of cynicism a journalist needs when he has lived through a revolution like ours, which you need to preserve and nurture like a secret and wild love affair. Cynicism feeds on doubt, incredulity and, above all, despair.

I'd had my fill of all three when I met Pedro Sánchez—the Tampico Man. And he looked like enough of a Holy Joe for me not to like him, at least by the way he acted. There was also such a clumsy scam about the character he played. A real Tampico man would never lisp his "cees" like that. So you might say it was not love at first sight between us.

I was a failure as a writer, not only as a poet but also as a reporter—the same guy who *El Heraldo* sent to cover the street during the labor movement, which was strong back then, instead of giving a decent editorial desk the benefit of my talents.

To make matters worse, I was living with the aid of a quart glass decanter, and neither did I avoid hanging around Dolores Street* to sink into sweet opium dreams, while that

---

Translator's note: Mexico City's Chinatown.

damned Tampico Man just smoked cigars—and even then just once in a while—and felt guilty about it when he did, too.

I'd heard about him, and seen him from a distance a couple of times until the Palacio de Hierro strike broke out, when a quirk of fate brought us together as if we had bumped into each other in a blind alley.

I had taken a taxi, making like I was in a rush, and hoping the accounts desk would pay me back if the events warranted it. I had hopes the business would hit the big time, and the CGT rarely let me down. For them, strikes were an all or nothing battle for the organization as a whole. I had just published a short piece the day before on how a strike had broken out at the Palacio de Hierro's workshops after a foreman had mistreated the seamstresses. That's why I was getting out of the taxi the day after when the fun and games began. The workers were picketing the negotiations and wouldn't let a dozen scabs get past. A whole truckload of gendarmes turned up with a water cannon in tow, which they used to spray a group of women on picket duty who had kids in their arms. Just like that. Then stones began to fly at the firemen when the gendarme officer, José Moriá, alias El Chato, gave the order to open fire on the workers. Then the Tampico Man went into action. He pulled away from the stone throwers as the first shots were fired, then, with his hand in his pocket, he went toward the lieutenant who'd given the order to fire.

"Aren't you ashamed to fire on unarmed workers?" he shouted, and just kept on walking toward him.

"But the stones, they're throwing stones..."

"Because they've got nothing else, you gobshit," and stood one step away from the lieutenant, who was reaching for his pistol. The Tampico Man grabbed the man's hand with his free hand, keeping the other one in his pocket, and whispered something to him. The gendarmes had forgotten about the strikers because they were watching the duel between that man and the lieutenant. For a moment, I waited for the shot so I could write down in my notebook how a worker had been murdered in cold blood by a lieutenant of the gendarmes. But nothing happened. Everything went quiet. The strikers fell back, taking two wounded with them, the firemen had fled with the stone-throwing, leaving their armored car and water cannon behind. The Tampico Man stepped away from the officer, facing him all the time, moving sideways, which made him pass right by my side.

"What d'you say to him?"

"For you or for the paper?"

"For the paper."

"Like 'How dare you fire on unarmed workers? Have you got shares in the Palacio de Hierro, or something'?"

"No, tell me what really happened."

The Tampico Man came up to me and showed me the hand he had kept in his greatcoat pocket, and the cocked .45 in it.

"I showed him my little friend here, and swore by his mother—because mine's already dead—that if he didn't calm down, he'd have three bullets in his guts and Satan'd be tanning his arse in hell."

And without waiting for me to say anything, he went straight back to the strikers.

I have a lot of respect for bravery or madness, but I have a lot more for effectiveness, and that phony Tampico Man won me over with that one. And the rest was secondary—that he slept on benches in the streetcar drivers' union, that he owned nothing, borrowed everything and never gave it back to who had lent it to him but to the first person he came across, that he knew all of Góngora or Quevedo's poetry by heart, and spoke English, Spanish, French and Turkish. He had another thing going for him—he never asked or did any favors. Just doing things the way he did, he got people to lend him books, buy him coffee, show him the way or take conversations the way he wanted them to.

Even then, I wouldn't have ended up liking him were it not for the mocking way he treated himself. Not the way I treat myself, which barely masks the self-contempt I sometimes have. It was something else, something difficult to explain.

"I'm a lousy character, a ham actor in an amazing play, mate. The play is important, but we're just second-rate actors, extras, puppeteers."

"You—and this is what really fucking bothers me—believe in destiny," I was saying to him as we sat back in the only sofa I had in my place, the only one the loan sharks had left. It was a stupid pink sofa, with mother-of-pearl buttons sewn into it, and an armrest between the two occupants.

"I reckon that people who build houses don't live in them. But I don't think that's any reason to stop building them, do you?"

"Enough of the rhetoric, you lousy Spanish bastard," I would say to him.

"Don't run away from the flame inside you, you shitty hack," he would answer me back.

"You go around looking for the bullet that's going to free you from living. Your stuff is religion, punishment, penitence. You've got the soul of a Christian, like the ones they used to throw to the lions."

"I came to the world through love and by chance. I want to leave it the same way—through love and by chance," he would answer. "What's Christian about believing in chance?"

"We men just go and blow everything. Everything. We're really good at destroying things, but not so hot at building them," I would say.

"This is how it is—you go to a harbor and there are three steamers waiting. You want to travel, you want to move, you want to be at one with the world, you want to live. One of the steamers says 'To Hell'; another one says 'Exploitation, Trickery, Capital.' And the other says 'Social Revolution.' You either stay in the harbor and watch the ships steam away with your baggage on one of them— you don't know which—or you make up your mind and get on board."

"You're probably right, but what's the point in being right? We're talking about life."

We used to run into each other by chance, sometimes three times a week. He would sleep in my bed, while I slept on the awful pink sofa. Sometimes I wouldn't see him for two months at a time.

Once he went away, walking through the rain, and after borrowing a book off me. He never gave it back.

30

Maybe all I have managed to imagine correctly about that cellophane-wrapped thing called the future is your funeral.

I can see your coffin being carried shoulder-high along an avenue running down to the coast (in Tampico? Gijón? Shanghai? Rotterdam? New Orleans?) to be cast into the sea, and left to sink slowly. Just a small procession, made up of tried and trusted friends, with a few black flags flapping in the breeze.

31

"Well, bugger me sideways, it's a Titian," San Vicente said, looking at the painting above the safe.

"You're obviously a connoisseur," the owner of the Imperial Mill replied. He was tied to a beige brocade armchair while he was being robbed.

"If you don't tell me the combination, it'll take me three hours to open that safe. It's an '18 Bereter-Zima. It'll be quite a job," San Vicente said, walking around the room, looking at the furnishings and the drapes. El Chato sat in the matching chair opposite the Imperial owner, carelessly waving a pistol at him. He looked quite sinister with a red mask over his face—a hood with a slit cut for his eyes—though he had forgotten to make a mouth-hole to smoke through.

"I swear to you I don't know," the company boss said. "Furthermore, even if I did know, there's only stocks and worthless documents in there. There's no money."

"How come you don't know, if it's your safe?" San Vicente asked him.

"I forgot because I'm frightened," the man said, very seriously.

"We'll do something about opening it and getting hold

of the factory payroll which you've had in there for the last two weeks since the strike started and which you use to pay scab labor and pay the chief of the mounted police to fuck the strikers around. We're going to do something about that. We're going to inject petrol through the door with a syringe, then we'll burn the whole bloody lot, including your Titian. Like the village idiot said, 'If it ain't for my church, it ain't for no one.' And he burned the whole thing down."

"You're crazy, sir."

"Hey, mate," San Vicente said to El Chato. "Bring the ingredients, will you?"

"If you swear to me you won't give the money to the workers, I'll tell you the combination."

"Remembered now, have you?" San Vicente asked him while he pretended that El Chato had handed a syringe to him and was fiddling with the safe behind the owner's back.

"O.K., O.K., I've remembered. Just swear to me..."

"Damn you. Not only don't you deserve the Titian, you don't even deserve to be left in one piece."

"Six to the right..." the factory owner said, while San Vicente carefully put out the blowtorch he had brazenly lit up so as not to burn the painting which wasn't to blame for anything.

32

There are 52 San Vicentes and 31 Sanvicentes in the Mexico City phone directory. That does not mean a great deal. There are 39 pages of Sánchez in tight eight-point type, and I have not so much as dared to count the number of Gonzálezes or Pérezes. And so it was I began early one Sunday morning.

"Excuse me, is this the San Vicente family house?"

"..."

"I know this may seem a little strange, but I'm a writer trying to find out about a Mr. San Vicente who lived in Mexico City in the twenties."

"..."

"No, from Gijón, in Spain."

"Oh, I see, your grandparents were from Torreón. No, thank you very much. You're grandfather was in the Revolution? Yes, really, but the San Vicente I'm looking for was..."

33

FROM THE MINUTES:
Item seven on the agenda. General
business. Sánchez proposes that, along
with rational education, Swedish
gymnastics be adopted as a principle of
social and cultural life in the unions.
Castro, Pedro and Cervantes, Luis oppose
the motion as one matter does not have
the same importance as the other.
Sánchez takes off his jacket, vest and
pants, and gives a demonstration in his
underwear. The assembly votes 11-2
against (namely, Pedro Sánchez, and the
undersigned, the assembly secretary). In
protest at the lack of consideration by
those present for their arguments,
Sánchez and García, Pedro walk out of the
meeting in their underwear to carry on
demonstrating the virtues of Swedish
gymnastics in the union local doorway to
any workers passing by.

Yours in Health and Social Revolution,

(signed)
Pedro García

cc: Cervantes, Luis.

34

To the relevant authorities:

Officer Marcial Ramos Mejía, attached to
Precinct VII in Mexico City, and at the
request of his superior officer, Captain
Leonardo Márquez Lacroix, hereby informs
the authorities of the events that occurred
today between 4:00 and 6:30 p.m.
    The undersigned had been commissioned
together with nine other agents from his
group to keep a surveillance watch on
the General Workers' Confederation local
at No. 27 Uruguay Street, hoping that
the Spanish subversive José San Vicente,
error, Sebastián San Vicente, a.k.a.
Pedro Sánchez, a.k.a. the Tampico Man
would show up, since he is on our wanted
list. Although he was deported from
Mexico last year, he has returned to
continue with his illegal activities,
according to information from our
captain. We took up positions at the
scene of these events about 4 p.m. and

discreetly began surveillance thereafter. We saw the subject mentioned enter about 6 p.m. together with six subjects from the streetcar drivers' union on our files. The identification, made by the undersigned and two accompanying agents (No. 1103 and No. 876), was confirmed by photographs made available to us of the subject taken at the time of his deportation. So as not to waste time, as they say, we got in touch with the seventh precinct, who sent us two trucks with 24 armed policemen. As we could not find the captain, the group under my command entered the above-mentioned union local going up the stairs and knocking down the entrance, error, door. A streetcar drivers' union assembly was in progress, attended by 200, error, 300 of its members. As we entered and in spite of our re-spectful requests that they put their hands up, many of those present jumped on us more with the aim of attacking than interfering as one agent (No. 1123) sighted the above-mentioned San Vicente entering the bathroom, error, the door we later discovered was to the bathroom. We made our way after a struggle with those present (find enclosed a list of unionists and agents wounded) and the undersigned lost a belt buckle and received a black eye for using our firearms as ordered. The undersigned was the one who had to force the bathroom door which was locked from inside as he had ascertained previously, and was then surprised to find nobody inside and San Vicente vanished. The bathroom is a single room, 4 ft. x 3 ft. with a flush toilet and a washbasin in a considerable unwashed state. Only ventilation is a small window 10 (ten) inches wide by 15 (fifteen) inches high located above toilet. The window at the local is on the third floor and looks out onto a yard. Tests were done to see if anybody could get through, and it was deemed impossible. In view of this the agent who said he sighted San Vicente entering bathroom (No. 1123) was punished, although the latter defended himself by saying the door was locked from the inside. Given that the entrance to the local was under surveillance by several agents and nobody left and a thorough search was made of all present, there is nothing more to report.

Officer Ramos Mejía (No. 978)

(At the foot of the page, a handwritten note in pencil "Bust down to private for being a jerk," and an illegible signature)

35

He was cleaning his two weapons—the black anodized Browning caliber .25 automatic and the .32 caliber Colt police special. He got the former as a present in Atlixco, and he was paid the latter in kind by the owner of a downtown gun store—he repaired the boiler in the building, the owner gave him the gun. He cleaned them once a week, placing the parts on a piece of chamois leather and cleaning them.

There was a plate with leftovers next to the chamois leather on the table where the debates were chaired. A column of ants crawled between the revolver cylinder and the loose bullets, carrying bits of bread with them. San Vicente smiled at them as he oiled his guns.

36

He uses the raindrops sliding down the window—which he wets his fingertips with—to comb his hair. She crosses the street, crying, two floors below, bumping into people walking the opposite way. She staggers, quickens her pace to jump over a puddle, and is almost run over by a green Packard, which then emits shouts and guffaws. He draws away from the window where he has been waiting for her for two hours and goes into the bathroom. He meticulously washes his hands to get rid of the last traces of oil from the engine he has been working on, and then he goes to the door. She is there waiting when he opens it. She sinks her head into his vest and soaks it with her tears and the rain dripping from her hair. He tries to look into her eyes, but she hides them from him, digging them into the top button on his gray vest.

"Why can't we be like everybody else?" she asks, but he does not hear her whispered tones too well, and he thinks she said, "Where's everybody else?" So he answers, "How do you mean, everybody else?" "The rest," she says to him. "Anybody else," she goes on. He does not understand. He strokes the rain-flattened curls on her forehead as he pushes the door shut. So again she says, "Why can't we be like everybody else?" He realizes what she had meant to say and answers, "It would all be so awful." But he also realizes there is a bit more than the rhetoric of defeated people in the phrase, and he looks at her carefully.

She huddles up close to him, shelters herself there, her hair—unintentionally nuzzled under his hook nose—smelling of rain. There—standing in the doorway to the room, lit up by a dim oil lamp that barely sheds light for ten feet around it—they seem like a pair of awkward actors who have forgotten their lines and are waiting for the prompter to give them back the magic of the stage and the curtain call. He strokes her back and feels how it arches in pain. "What's wrong?" he asks her, as she untangles herself from the embrace and moves out of the halo of light and over to the cot where San Vicente sleeps, which is now covered with newspapers that have wrenches and copper pipes all over them. As she cannot collapse onto the cot, she sits on the corner.

She is away from the lamplight now. He senses where she is, sniffling in the darkness. He comes closer with the Coleman lamp in his hand, and he begins to carefully pick up his work tools, putting the newspapers down on the floor, then placing the solder, machine parts and rusty nuts and bolts on top of them. She takes advantage of the cleared space and stretches out along the cot, her boots get tangled up in the sheets and they smear mud on them. The hems of her long black skirt are threadbare, her boots hide her darned stockings, and her shawl is patched up. The more he looks at her, the more worn out she seems. There are two blood-stained lines that tremble on her white blouse as she sobs with her face buried in the pillow. He goes over to the kitchen, set up in a corner of the room, and picks a coffee pot up from an oil-burning stove, pours water into an empty coffee cup, and picks a rag of doubtful cleanliness up from a bedside table.

"Don't tear my blouse, it's the only one I've got," she says. "And it washes well." He helps her to unbutton her sleeves and take her blouse off, carefully picking it off her bloodstained parts. Her pointed, ample breasts wobble freely. She has got two cuts on her back, long gashes with blood seeping through the broken skin. "Who the hell did this to you?" he asked. "What does it matter?" she answers as he wets the kitchen cloth in the cup and carefully cleans her cuts. He bites his lips. A couple of tears well up in his eyes and run down his face before falling into the cup.

37

At the request of his friend José Rojas—one day as they are sleeping in the railroad station as the rain pours down monotonously, the smell of grass lingers in the air, and a couple of dogs approach them to share in the warmth— San Vicente recites Calderón de la Barca.* He knows all of Segismundo's monologues in "Life is a Dream" by heart. Every last bit of them.

Translator's note: Famous sixteenth century Spanish playwright. Segismundo is a leading character in the play "La vida es sueño," usually translated as "Life is a dream."

38

A man came limping along with the news, which he had gotten from a kid keeping watch outside the Indianilla works—the streetcars were running, driven by scabs and with army escorts! A roar broke out around the assembly hall and reverberated along the corridors and spilled out onto Uruguay Street, where over 2,000 CGT activists had gathered, including more than 1,000 striking streetcar drivers. San Vicente did not wait for the shouts to die down but ran down the stairs along with the echoes. He was wearing blue overalls and a railroad worker's cap, which covered his face down to his eyebrows.

Just as he was leaving the building, a speaker was leaning out of a window, rousing the workers crowded on the sidewalks and most of the street. San Vicente went over to the streetcar rails that came within ten yards of the union local and sat down on top of one of them. He had his hand in his pocket, stroking the barrel of his pistol, unaware of the ache of metal that was burning in the palm of his hand.

It was 11:15 on a cloudy morning. The first streetcar—a motorized one, No. 798—with a car in tow, had left the depot at eleven and went through the Plaza de Armas a few minutes later. There were no passengers on board because nobody had felt like stopping it. A scab was driving it escorted by eight soldiers—all Yaqui Indians armed with Mausers—from the palace guards regiment. The streetcar turned onto Uruguay Street at 11:18.

San Vicente drew his pistol and stood up between the rails, a dozen streetcar workers at his side. The motorized car slowed down, and one of the Yaquis shot at one of the men who had not moved out of the way. The shot went overhead and, as the streetcar braked to a halt, stones and glass filled the air. The escort party shot back. A Mauser bullet went through a two-volume edition of *Don Quixote* in a bookstore across from the union office. A piece of stone shrapnel sliced the finger off a sixteen-year-old weaver who was leaning against the wall, three yards from the union's doorway.

San Vicente cocked his pistol but was not the first to act. Roberto Etagere, a streetcar worker, took a running jump and threw himself through a streetcar window and wrestled a Mauser off one of the soldiers. Then he shot the scab who was driving. San Vicente jumped through the door opposite. Rifle shots flew around inside the streetcar. The Spaniard fired off six shots at the soldiers, wounding three of them. The streetcar windows were shattered, and the air was filled with shards of glass that cut the hands and faces of the crowd that had grabbed hold of the car to try and turn it over.

Four soldiers ran out of the back door, but were engulfed in a jostling crowd that stripped them of their rifles and cartridge belts. Some more streetcars turned the corner, three at least, and all with escorts. The crowd received them with rifle and pistol fire. The soldiers took refuge at the corner of Uruguay and Bolívar, making a barricade with a streetcar and a horse-drawn cart that had been delivering coal and had been requisitioned.

The CGT activists opened fire from doorways every time a soldier appeared. They could not do the same from the union local because they had to lean too far out of the windows, and that didn't make sense. Nonetheless, some comrades climbed onto the rooftops and opened fire with two Mausers they had snatched from the soldiers in the first car that had come along. Gunshots were exchanged for over ten minutes. Word was passed around that pistols were not to be used until the soldiers attempted to charge, so the shooting was sporadic, and most of the workers stayed under cover inside the local or in neighboring doorways. Another barricade was formed on the opposite corner, using sacks of coffee from a store.

Then, suddenly, everything changed. Arnulfo González, military district commander, came up San Juan Letrán with a double column of armed gendarmes, who were trying to charge their way through. At least a hundred pistols opened fire at once from inside the building and its doorways. In the windows on the second floor, a group of telephone workers—led by Flora Padilla, Arturo Rojo, Moisés Guerrero and the Alcalá brothers—were trying out their aim. Several gendarmes fell, the rest ran away.

Those workers without pistols ran away over the rooftops or down the unblocked street. Three hundred workers were left to defend the street and the union, almost all of them armed. San Vicente, taking advantage of the chaos, advanced along with three streetcar workers—Clemente Mejía, alias the She-Wolf, Ramón Estrada, alias the Skunk, and José Salgado, alias Grandpa—toward the barricade, yelling and shooting all the while. The gendarmes retreated a block before the charge, but there the CGT activists were held back by rifle fire.

After taking two of the barricades, the besieged workers managed to catch some breath. San Vicente ran toward the local. Durán, from the weavers' union, and Moisés Gutiérrez, from the Palacio de Hierro union, appeared to have taken charge of the defense.

"This is a matter of ammunition. We won't be able to hold the local for very long," Durán said.

"What if we get away over the rooftops?" San Vicente suggested.

"Then what?"

"Then we have a general strike."

"The general strike's already been called. The unarmed comrades who went off are spreading the word around the factories."

"Then we wait."

"Everyone inside as soon as the barricades can't hold out any more. We can hang on a bit more here. Pass it on."

And so they managed to stop a second charge from the gendarmes, but those who were manning the barricades had to abandon them for lack of ammunition.

The soldiers moved closer and closer to the building for the next hour. The defenders, watching their ammunition carefully, met each cautious move with gunfire.

San Vicente carefully took aim at an overbearing

gendarme officer giving two soldiers orders, and fired. The bullet went straight through the man's hand and he dropped to the ground. "I aimed at his shoulder," San Vicente said. It was his last bullet.

"Anyone got any .45 rounds to spare?" he asked.

Beside him, Riverol, a blacksmith, smiled and said, "I've been aiming without slugs for a while, just to pretend."

The gendarmes could be seen from the windows, regrouping for the next charge. If there were no bullets left, then they would soon be coming up the stairs. They could be held up for a while there, with two or three shots, bricks and a few benches.

"We'll surrender before the next charge. We've got just ten slugs between forty comrades up there," said Moisés Gutiérrez, who had come down from the upper floor. "Has anybody got a white shirt we can use as a flag?"

"Like hell we're surrendering," said Orestes, a black guy from Veracruz who worked in a laundry.

"How many shots you got left?"

"Two."

"O.K. Fire them, and that'll be all, because there's little we can do now."

"Shit," said San Vicente.

Magdalena Hernández' underskirts were used for the surrender flag. The unionists were then made to run the gauntlet between a double column of gendarmes, who hit them with rifle butts—246 were detained. They were then packed into buses requisitioned by the Gendarmerie colonel, and taken to the 7th Precinct headquarters. Charges were filed there. San Vicente gave a false name—Pedro

Sánchez—but the officer who wrote it down did not seem to mind at all. The gendarmes' casualties were six dead, 72 wounded. The workers lost one dead—a streetcar driver Manuel Roldán—and eleven wounded. The local had been overrun. The general strike did break out, but was confined to the textile mills in the south of the city, the telephone workers, and the Palacio de Hierro works. The streetcars, on the other hand, kept on working, driven by scab labor. The Finance Minister, Adolfo de la Huerta, intervened to have the unionists freed. So—72 hours later—they were released just as they had been taken in.

39

A friend, a comrade says to him, "Sebastián, normal men fall in love with a whore once in their lives, idealists spend time trying to reform them, but you couldn't stop there. No, you just had to go and organize them."

Sebastián San Vicente answers something about how everybody has the right to live, and how the workers' organization is the road toward making those rights count. His friend, his comrade, passes him a pork and purslane taco. San Vicente stares at it before eating it. This is his only defect regarding Mexican food—he has to stare at it before eating it, observe it closely before shoving it into his mouth. It does not matter whether he sees it, as he will eat it in any case—these are hungry times and he is not fussy. Or is he? Just fussy enough to stare at something he is about to eat. As he chews, Sebastián tells his friend:

"Don't call them whores. They're comrades now."

"Comrade whores, then," says his incorrigible friend.

40

San Vicente said:

"You know this isn't Rotterdam. But you only know that because your memory tells you so. Forget your memory for a moment. Forget you don't know Rotterdam and that, on the other hand, you know this city really well because you've lived here since you were a lad. Hang on a minute, just listen to me. Say to yourself: We're in Shanghai, we're about to disembark in Boston. That man there isn't wearing a straw hat, he's black, his head is uncovered. There isn't any half-arsed and not-so-Aristotelian sun, we're in Cape Town. You know what I mean, like? D'you get it? Don't you feel it in your bones? It's random, it's accidental, it's just scenery. Don't fall into the scenery trap, don't let scenery confuse you, or cloud your emotions, your feelings. Don't degrade your capacity for rational thought, don't let it get all murky because of that one-eyed woman looking at us, the one called Concha López. She's Greek and her name's Lydia, and she isn't one-eyed, she's one of those half-arsed dancers from a bar in Piraeus. Don't let yourself be kidded. You go through life, taking the scenery away. No, don't take the people away. That's not the point. Without people, you've got nothing, just shadows. Ideas without people are a load of shit. They're shitty shadows, streaks of piss on a streetlamp. No, that's not what I meant. I wanted to say it's the same thing—that scenery doesn't need to cloud your feelings, the capacity to seethe at the slightest injustice, seethe until you're on the verge of going mad, until you cough blood, until, as they say, you're like a mad dog... What does scenery matter to a mad dog, the enemy will say, and he'll be right. D'you get it?"

41

"But did this man exist or didn't he?" my publisher Marco Antonio Jiménez—who's really suspicious—asks.

"Of course he existed."

"But how do you tell his story?"

"I just go along, a few details here and there."

"Real details?"

"Well, are you going to publish it or not? What the fuck does it matter whether he was really like this or like that, whether his clothes were this color or that?"

"But did he exist?"

"Sure enough."

"Good."

42

How many hunchback friends have you got? I haven't got any. You haven't got any either, right? That's just what I thought. That's the problem. Nobody has hunchback friends. That Victor Hugo jerk took care of making everybody think hunchbacks are good guys who make assholes of themselves falling in love. Nobody wants friends like that. And nobody wants a hunchback called Leoncio del Prado y Jiménez, even if he does favors for free and works in a cathouse. So it went that I only had good relationships in the world, because as for friendship, real friendship, there was nothing doing, unless you count a blind librarian, a dog on the corner and this half-crazy whore they call Cramps. I'm telling you all this so you can see I don't have any friends, I don't make any friends, and I don't let people make friends with me either.

So you might say I'm not a soft touch as far as friendship goes, and San Vicente wouldn't have managed it, not even he, if it hadn't been because I felt sorry to see him the way he was that day, with a black eye all swollen up, an inch-long gash on his eyebrow, three broken ribs, pissing blood after they'd kicked him in the kidneys, and a toe facing the wrong way after they'd damned well busted it for him. On top of that, he was sleeping between two beds on the floor on some threadbare carpet while a pair of those whores were sleeping just fine and dandy on those fucking mattresses of theirs.

So I set to work and sorted things out straight off.

"Get up you pair of bitches, or I'll fuck the pair of you at once!"

The threat worked and I had both beds free for San Vicente there and then.

"Thanks, comrade," San Vicente said, as I bandaged his ribs and put one of the whore's corsets on top of the bandages.

Then he said to me, "You look bright, so either I'm really mistaken or that spark in your eye means you know a lot about life—shit—because intelligence isn't something you're born with, like some jumped-up johnny-come-lately creeps say as if—Christ, that hurts!—you didn't have to work at it. I'll bet you've read something by Malatesta."

"Move yourself over to the right a bit. My right, not yours. Malatesta, most of Bakunin, Kropotkin, Grave, Flores Magón and a complete collection of *La Protesta* sent to me specially from Buenos Aires, which I do not lend out because they don't come back; the whores just wipe their asses with them, and such lovely texts were not meant for such scabby asses."

"I knew it—ahhh—I knew it—ahhh, ahhh," said San Vicente, who was stoic but only up to a point. It must have hurt him like hell when I was trying to straighten his broken toe.

"I'll tell you right now, because we may not have the chance to talk again," he said very seriously, and I left the last tweak on the bandage until he'd finished his speech. "You may be hunchbacked, pug-nosed or even from

Asturias—that's just the luck of the draw—but what matters is what you think. The rest is just appearances, ethereal form, an accident of fate, chance."

"I already knew that," I answered him.

"Great. Ohh, ohh! Right then, we don't have to kid each other—you with your hunchback and me with my hernia and flat feet. We're above these things."

"That's a good start. You're a gentleman," I told him.

"'Gentlemen' usually have money, comrade," he answered.

I left him to doze a while and went out to organize a scientific alarm system that would cover all three floors of the cathouse, the entire street and a few blocks around. I'm just that sort, because even if I never ask for favors, I certainly give them out all the time. It's not for nothing that I'm the only hunchback with a medical diploma from the Sorbonne who treats people for free in the Bolsa district, who practices abortions, cures bleeding runaways, watches out for venereal diseases and quack herbal remedies. All that, and preventive medicine, selling condoms at cost, curing skin diseases and curing uncontrollable drug and alcohol addiction using the Prado method where if the patients don't die, it's a cinch they're saved for the rest of their vice-free days.

San Vicente slept the clock round without any help from laudanum, and woke up facing the usual hodgepodge of riff-raff who lived in Madame Concha's place—in other words, me, the dog, my friend Cramps, two Swiss whores whom the locals called Milly and Molly because they were twins, and Madame Concha herself, who wanted to know when she would get the room with two beds back.

"Don't you worry about me, I'll be off right away. Thanks a lot for putting me up," said San Vicente right away.

Just then Cramps did one of her more celebrated numbers of that time, which was making one of her breasts pop out with just one twitch of a muscle. San Vicente stared at her and smiled.

"Admirable bust, Miss, it's a pleasure to see it."

"No, no, you don't have to go, Sebastián. You know you're at home here," Madame Concha said—she was not normally like that with guests. "But I do need you to move into the attic so the girls can use their room."

We wrapped him up in the carpet and all of us, even the dog, helped to carry him two floors up to a room that hadn't been used much since General Murguía rose up in arms at the wrong time and got the firing squad for it. It was a room that Murguía's second-in-command, Colonel Torres—who was shot too—had decorated according to his own tastes: black walls and a white four-poster bed. It was too morbid for regular clients.

"Well, I reckon it's time for introductions," San Vicente said, when the court circle that had gathered to carry him up retired, leaving us alone. A shaft of sunlight came through a patch of glass where the black paint had peeled off.

"Leoncio del Prado y Jiménez, M.D.—from Zacatecas."

"Sebastián San Vicente, naval mechanic—originally from Gijón."

"I'd heard of you hereabouts. You have a lot of friends among the young ladies that work in this flophouse... Something to eat?"

"Doctor, I'm sorry to tell you I haven't a peso to my

name, and I don't suppose I will for a couple of weeks and, what's more, I don't acknowledge debts for food as I consider that to be an obligation between human beings."

"That's how I see things too," I told him and went to fetch him some chicken broth from a diner two blocks from the cathouse. The owner had served me for free since I cured him of a particularly virulent case of scabies, which not only had him really fucked up but was scaring his customers away, too.

San Vicente seemed to be keener on questions when he had the cup of broth in his hands.

"Forgive me for interfering with your life, but curiosity killed the cat, as they say. I know it's all the same asking a man like you how he came to be in such a state, as asking me why I'm a hunchback. You'll just say: it's destiny, as I would, but..."

"Do you want to know, Doctor, or do you want to explain it to me?"

"..."

"The CROM couldn't find any other way to move into the La Colmena works than hiring a bunch of unemployed men—unemployed cops sacked from El Oro—and put them under the command of a friend of Alvarez, a slob of a leader from the Mexico City Federation, whom even they had sent to Coventry because he had got addicted to drugs and was of no use, not even as an office worker. So he told a fat bloke called Macías, 'Retake La Colmena and you'll get your old job back.' So off Macías went getting the gang together—gave them money, guns and set them to work. Then he spoke to the Barróns and assured them he'd clean all the anarchists out of the factory, and they were pleased as Punch since they wouldn't even have to pay for it, just turn a blind eye to things and call the police as soon as the police were needed. So that's when the trouble started. First, the company contracted half-a-dozen of Macías' men, who started to stir things up in the shops... And our people, who are anything but patient, took things into their own hands and then there were shoot-outs on the way out, lone comrades beaten up, guards beaten up, a strike in response to it all, and so on. That's why I had to get involved. Also, it had to be someone like me, an outsider, who wouldn't get the comrades into trouble, who would just turn up, do what had to be done, and disappear."

"What did you do?"

"Anything. Don't put that admiring look on your face, Doctor, it makes me nervous. You know what courage is? Of course, you know very well. Courage is doing what you don't have to when they say you don't have to, and then facing the music. Courage has nothing to do with fear. Fear is always with you, it keeps you good company. Fear stops you from going mad and doing something stupid, fear stops everything coming for free. It's fear that lends importance to actions, that makes situations responsible. If I wasn't scared, I'd be a pleasant fool..."

"So what did you do?"

"I went to the place where Macías gets together with his cronies—on top of a dive in the Tlalpan district, on the second floor. I went in and told them..."

"What did you tell them?"

"Fuck it all. What could I say to them...? There were

seven of them, counting Macías. What was I supposed to say? 'Here's the representative of the proletariat, you bastards...?' Or, 'Don't you realize that, as sons of the working class, you're destroying your own future, carrying on like that for a scab organization set up by the bosses?' So I said, 'Good evening. They told me you could give me a job.' And Macías answered me, 'What kind of a job?' And as I saw he was right by the window, I said, 'The job to do with...' and pushed him straight out. Still, he was brawny as well as fat, the fat sod, and didn't drop out just like that. So I really shoved him and down he went, breaking glass and all, all two floors of it..."

"What did his sidekicks do?"

"Them? Nothing."

"???"

"Because Fatso Macías wanted to take someone with him, so he grabbed my jacket on the way down, and so he took me down with him, all two floors of it."

"What happened to the fat guy?"

"Doctor, if you want to treat him, you'll need to look in your trunk for some other diplomas apart from those you got at the Sorbonne because when I left the place he was in a very sorry state... What do I know? I suppose he must have died. And so that was the end of that episode in the life of La Colmena because no one's going to get that band together again without Fatso playing the tune for them to dance to, and giving them money and a good time..."

How did San Vicente know I kept my diploma in a trunk?

For the next two days, I spent my time treating him and

seeing if we had anything else in common—he didn't play chess nor bridge or believe in games of chance; he liked music but couldn't play the guitar; he knew Shakespeare's plays, but not his sonnets; he knew a lot about geography, tons of history, but nothing about natural sciences; he was well versed as a mechanic, could speak English, a bit of French, a bit of German and, I don't know how on earth he did, but he also spoke some Tagalog. He was a movie buff and foresaw that they would become the greatest show on earth as soon as they had sound and color.

I had the chance to study his approach to women during those two days. He was very direct, but gentle in his dealings, a bit sweet, but not syrupy, wanting to make everything clear (he was young, he lacked experience—since when can you make everything clear?) before taking the next step. Perhaps what my neighbors most liked about him was that he treated them like fairy-tale princesses. I watched him, trying to learn from his instincts.

He once told me, "Doctor, you've got to change your approach to women. If you stop thinking of them as things, some of them, the best ones, will stop thinking of you as a hunchback and see you as I do, as another human being, a very good doctor, well-educated and very agreeable."

I have followed his advice through thick and thin these last years. It never worked, but it was too late to take it up with San Vicente, because one day he went out to buy cigarettes and just vanished from our lives.

43

"Breaking the law has got to do with all aspects of life," he said. "But it has to be a lot of people breaking the law, a crowd."

"The idea is to live outside the law. Yourself, living outside the law," his friend José Rojas answered.

"No, I've got nothing against burgling a jewelry store to raise funds for the organization. I just think those funds could cost the organization very dear if the police find out," San Vicente said. "So yourself breaking the law should be weighed up against how much damage it can do to the rest." And that said, the problem was settled and he never spoke about it again.

44

San Vicente found out that the police dragnet was getting tighter. It all had to do with numbers. There were more and more stool pigeons at the meetings he usually went to. A light burning in the bathroom of a house meant danger; two policemen who just happened to be sleeping in the doorway he walked out of; friends who told him questions were being asked about him; an article in a newspaper warning that the "dangerous anarchist" had been sighted; a face in the middle of a demonstration that bore him no goodwill; certain traces of misgiving when he went to a house where he had been asked to come to dinner (nothing surly, nothing aggressive, just the textile worker looking across at the door more times than he ought to). That's what it was in the end—numbers. But maybe it was something else, just a certain I-don't-know-what in the air, as his poet friend would say. A certain I-do-know-what, San Vicente would say, who was a bit shrewder when it came to discerning clues in the air, as if there was fear about, as if it were going to rain and the air were charged with electricity and got denser for just a second, as if someone was crying on a far-off corner at night.

So that is how, that time, he came to sleep in Krone's circus, surrounded by animal cages.

"I come here too, when I can't sleep," said his friend Bruce, who tamed bears and Bengal tigers.

"No, no. I come here when I want to sleep."

"Today's not a good day. There's a full moon and the tigers are restless. The she-bear's got a toothache, too. You're not going to sleep well."

"I've got a headache, and they say I snore when I sleep outside so I hope I don't disturb your animals," San Vicente told him.

Bruce laughed. He was tall, the son of a Canadian father and a Tarahumara Indian mother from Chihuahua, with a mop of red hair, and prominent, copper-colored cheekbones. He was living on the edge, because his half-baked love for a trapeze artist brought out the dark side of him, and made him depressed and melancholy.

San Vicente stayed close to the tiger cage, staring right into the eyes of a 15-year-old Bengal tigress named Helena.

The smell of dried animal dung and wet straw, the tigress' growls as she rattled the cage now and again, hid all the other things in the air—that they were after him and closing in all the time.

45

Colonel Ramos told me, "Arrest him. If that damned Spaniard is still in Mexico, he's all yours. What the hell does that asshole think we are, some kind of joke? He's all yours, Gómez, all yours. But if things don't turn out, I can already see you sweeping out the stables. This is an order, and it comes direct from the General, the Minister himself. Use whatever resources you like."

Gómez, that's me. Arturo Gómez, captain in the Mexico City mounted police. Shot my way up to Captain, rather than getting here by picking up housebreakers or punks who mug old women. A frustrated pianist too, if you must know. I don't mean frustrated by lack of time or talent, but because I had two fingers blown off my left hand in the Battle of Celaya,* and nobody composes piano pieces for just the right hand.

So then, Gómez—in other words, me—went to his office and sat down in front of the file, and—since it was nighttime and I was supposed to be off duty—I took a bottle of El

---

Translator's note: Battle in 1915 which marked the ascendancy of Obregón's forces, and the decline of Pancho Villa's.

Caballito mezcal out of the desk drawer and began to read. Because Gómez—in other words, me—isn't any old jerk you can just order around: *Arrest this guy, grab this one's balls* and he goes right ahead. Gómez is a 28-year-old who's seen a lot of other people's blood spilt, as well as some of his own, who's in the police force by chance, and doesn't just do something without first having a good idea of what's expected from his action, who's expecting it, and why.

And so Gómez finds this San Vicente's file to be slippery like nobody's business—not lacking in courage and manhood, good for a shoot-out, and determined to grind the Mexican Revolution to dust with his crazy anarchist antics. He was no asshole, no murderer, nor a criminal of the sort I had suddenly found myself running into these last two years. He was worse and better than that. He was an idealist. We had already let him give us the slip twice. Mother fucker! What a bunch of jerks the Mexico City foot and mounted police and the reserves were, including Colonel Ramos, apart from Gómez—in other words, me. Twice we had our hands on him: once when we deported him in May 1921, and he came back to us; the other time a few months back, during the shoot-out on Uruguay Street. There it was in black and white—"Sánchez, Pedro"—on the list of those arrested and released a couple of days after. I began to take notes on a yellowing notepad, and when I had filled a page, I went to sleep well cured by the mezcal of the sorrows in my body and heart.

The following day, Gómez, bright-eyed and bushy-tailed but with no spurs on—as he was just going to do office work—turned up for duty at the precinct and began to fire out orders like a Maxim machine gun, like the ones the Austrians used to use, because I'm real good at that, rattling off orders that sound good and as if there's some point to them.

"I want to speak to reserve officer Ventura, Corporal. Right now!"

"Tell officers Marcial and Sousa to get here before I can say shit!"

"Who's the guy who's in charge of the stool-pigeons who sends us these pig-assed reports? Leyva? Get him here on the fuckin' double!"

"This file has a photo, but no copies. Where are the copies it says should be here? Get fifty made for me this morning. I don't give a damn if the Colonel wants pictures of his daughter's wedding! Tell him to go and get the guy with the cardboard horses in the Alameda to take them for him!"

"Get me the officer in charge of the San Angel precinct before I finish this cigarette I'm smoking!"

It wasn't too hard. The city wasn't so big then, and the problem was just to get your hand around it and squeeze it into a fist. San Vicente would be in there, somewhere.

Ventura came into the office an hour later, with his shirt-tails hanging out and his suit covered in grease stains.

"Just look at you, Ventura, you look like one of the bad guys, the ones we have to arrest. You could really do with spending a few months at headquarters although we'd have to cripple you to get you into military shape."

"Wrap it up, Captain, I'm not in a good mood. I had to spend all night following one of the Turk's gang, and spent it all in places where they drink pure piss."

"Looks like it."

"What am I good for?" he asked me.

"You arrested San Vicente on Uruguay Street in February. What's he like?"

"I can't really remember, because I arrested him, and then again I didn't arrest him. I mean, I didn't realize it at the time."

"But your people have had tabs on him. What do you know about him?"

Ventura got a couple of cigars out from his shabby suit, offered me one, and lit up when I declined. He looked at my collection of miniature cannons as he spoke.

"They protect him—that bunch of bastards from the factories. He's got no home, no wife, no job and he never sleeps in the same place twice. A jewel. You could find him if you took a bit of interest in some union assembly or other. Or we could have found him—who knows now?—if we hadn't already put out a red alert after so many failed attempts to pick him up. It's difficult to pick him up without getting into a shoot-out with lead flying all over the place. Are you authorized to provoke an incident with the CGT? Are you authorized to leave two or three dead and start a general strike, Captain?"

He left me thinking—so that's how it was.

"Which union locals does he normally go to, and at what time?"

"I can tell you that in no time. Just let me get over to the office and I'll send you a note with the details you asked for."

That said, he got up from his chair very ceremoniously, as if to say, "I'm passing you the buck, you jerk. You don't know what sort of trouble you're letting yourself in for." But I got the message all right.

I kept on thinking until the police photographer turned up—the one they'd made a sergeant so he wouldn't feel like such a jerk.

"At your service, Captain!"

"The photos. Don't beat about the bush, you brown-noser."

"Captain, I need two days to get you fifty photos of this San Vicente, and just look. He doesn't look too good in this photo you gave me, and the copies will be even worse... And the Colonel gave me a job to do..."

"Fifty photos before the day is out, or you'll be cleaning horseshit from Company Six stables until you get to like the taste of caca!"

Having solved that problem, I then faced Leyva, who was rolling his fat ass around on a bench outside the office, feeling very full of himself, the lazy bastard. Looking at him now, I realized why he ran informants—because he looked just like any old criminal. They loved the faggot, they must have really trusted him.

"You are a disgrace to your uniform. You smuggle tobacco, so I'm told. You smuggle whores into the barracks for junior officers, you deal in imported watches that must be stolen, and I don't know what else, Corporal Leyva," I told him straight off to soften him up. But you could see this was like water off a duck's back to him, because he just answered in a friendly way, "Anything I can do for you, Captain? Anything in particular?"

"You whoremongering bastard."

"A special price for you, Captain."

"Seven times round the yard, on the double! Jiménez!

Make sure Corporal Leyva carries out the order and then bring him back to me."

I supposed that would do some good because fat-assed Leyva—sweating out last night's booze at ten in the morning—would hardly be a tiger on the race track.

"Lieutenant Suárez at your service, Captain," said an elegant little officer, one of the new guard coming into the gendarmes because we had pretty uniforms. He must have spent the Revolution busy sucking his mother's tits.

"I have half an idea that this guy we're looking for, called San Vicente, spends the night in different houses in San Angel or Tizapán with textile workers who live out there. I want you to get this right and with discretion, not like your usual dumb-fuck, not like the charge of Pancho Villa."

"Did you fight with Villa, Captain?"

"No, Lieutenant. I whipped the asses of Villa's men at Celaya over and over until they got to like it... First, I want you to talk discreetly with the factory bosses out there. Discreetly—don't go kicking up a big stink. I want the addresses of all the main union men out there, the most active CGT members..."

"There must be about 500 of them, Captain."

"Never mind. You'll have to write a fucking lot. Then I want you to begin house searches at night—at night, you hear—under the pretext that we're looking for a robber, and that we do not think he's in their houses. You do the same next door until you find a man who looks like a mugshot I'll give you a bunch of tonight, one for each of the dummies under your command. No provocation, and no

arrests, even if they may be warranted. I don't want anybody behind bars because you found a gun or an under-
ground printing press. That's somebody else's business. I
just want this San Vicente guy. You got that?"

"Yes sir. When do we start the operation?"

"Tonight, or rather, go to San Angel and get the list. I'll
have the mug shots for you after eight. Split your company
up into two, and put yourself in charge of the group that's
going to carry out what I have asked you to do."

Well, that jerk wasn't going to catch so much as a cold,
but he'd smoke the fox out of his hole.

"Marcial and Sousa reporting for duty," said two shabby
gendarmes, who even had flies buzzing around them.

"How many shabby, ugly-looking bastards like your-
selves can you round up for me from the crack gendarmes
corps?"

"Boss, uh..." said Sousa, who had a way with words.

"Boss, uh..." said Marcial, who copied Sousa.

"Uh, a lot, or, uh, not many?"

"Uh..."

"Uh, shit-loads."

"Good. Bring six along at three this afternoon—out of
uniform. From now on, you have been commissioned for a
special job. You are going to do undercover work for a few
days. I want you to go around disguised as street vendors
from morning to night, observing union locals, to see if
you can find a guy and arrest him without making too much
fuss. I want the six of you here at two, disguised as street
vendors. And tonight you can stop by here to pick up the
list of places you must watch, photos of the guy you're

looking for and a list of more detailed instructions you'll have to learn by heart. Right then...move!"

I paused for breath. I'd earned it keeping that bunch of asses in line. I was into my second cigarette and my first mezcal when Leyva turned up, sweating and drooling like a pig.

"Here he is, Captain, about to have a heart attack," Officer Jiménez said with a smile from ear-to-ear.

"Leyva. As soon as you get over the healthy exercise I prescribed for you, I want you to run around town like the devil was after you. By tomorrow, I want to know where Sebastián San Vicente sleeps, where he's going to be in the next three hours, in the next five, the next day, in a week's time. He's a Spaniard with a hook nose, a well-known CGT man, goes by the name of Pedro Sánchez, and they call him the Tampico Man. Jiménez will give you a mug shot of him right here, tonight. You've got fifty pesos from the company cashier to pay your informants, but for each false lead or each time you rip me off, you'll go for a little run. Got that!?"

"Loud and clear, Captain."

Well then, mission accomplished. If we didn't get him now, the one running around the yard would be Captain Arturo Gómez—in other words, me.

46

You wake up amid screams. You jump out of your cot in your blue-and-gray striped prison-style pajamas with your gun in your hand—you've grabbed it from under your pillow. The floor is cold, and even though the world around you has turned into a carnival full of confusion, you try to get your bearings—figuring out where you are sleeping, which house you are in, where the doors lead to, and what streets are nearby. Because it is obvious that the people looking for you are moving in—those shouts and those confused orders and those rifle-butts smashing on doors leave no shadow of a doubt. You put your shoes on, without socks, and sling another revolver over your shoulder—you've checked that it's loaded.

"Come out, San Vicente, with your hands up!"

There is a window—you lean out. You can hear bullets tearing through the door behind you. First things first—you throw a five-foot wardrobe against the door, then the cot and a trunk full of old plates. The window. On the first floor. You stick your head out, your hair on end as if you had just had a fright. And what the hell is this if it isn't a fright? The glass shatters and a shot comes in through the window. The bullet smashes into the ceiling, raising a neat little cloud of plaster. You smash the remaining window-panes with the barrel of your colt, and rattle off five shots in quick succession. The rifle butts are now splintering the door. You jump out of the window. You lose a shoe when your feet hit the ground, and you keep on shooting—using the revolver now—at two shadows that go scurrying away. You reload by lamplight and then you run like a ghost in pajamas through the streets of San Angel, singing "Sons of the People" at the top of your voice, out of tune on the part that goes, *The red banner of liberty*... You think it would be better to sing Beethoven's *Ninth* in these unusual and tricky circumstances.

47

In Luigi Fabbri's biography of Malatesta, I find a note on top of the page I must have written in the late '60s: *What do we want the quiet of cafés for, if we already have the storm?* I suppose neither one is an accident, that it was written at the end of the '60s or that it is in a book about Malatesta. Nor is it an accident that it turns up 30 years later, when the time has come to explain why there was all this chasing after San Vicente.

Years ago, when I gathered together the odds and ends I had managed to find out about him, I wrote a ten-line newspaper article, saying something like this: "The author of these lines confesses that one of his latest obsessions revolves around reviewing and extending the Left's pantheon of heroes. The author remembers the difficulties the '68 generation had coming up with names and faces to appeal to in order to establish a vague thread of continuity, some red Grandpas to take us in..." These words may constitute personal clues: notes scribbled in the margins in a book about Malatesta, the book itself, a review for the pantheon of heroes... But the question itself begs more questions in turn: Why San Vicente? What does San Vicente embody? Could it just be stubbornness that makes him slip out of anonymity? Is it his dogged devotion to principles? Is it that consistency which makes him a harmonious character rather than one torn apart by contradictions? Or is it his absence of any sense of nationality?

I suppose there might be a bit of the last point buried underneath the cobwebs in the most remote recesses inside my head—the idea of voluntary exile, the idea that being rooted to a homeland is a piece of the many landscapes which you can feel as your own. Or it has to do with friends, experiences, situations, segments of a social class that are faceless but which you belong to anyway. It is not just an idea, an abstract thought, but a sensation of intimate affinity, of pleasure which you feel as warmth flowing through you as you walk through the Asturian mountains, near the mine entrances, or lose yourself in the dust in Irapuato, or hear experiences related in the pages of a book which sound frighteningly like your own. Things like the ones that have little to do with what your passport may say, because they have yet to invent a passport for each social class, bits of a region or scraps from a story. They have yet to invent "World Citizen" passports issued in Gijón. There is this crazy idea that San Vicente carried around with him during his three years in Mexico—the idea that revolution is just part of the baggage, is just a part of the personal jigsaw puzzle that went along slotting itself into jigsaw puzzles lodged in many cities, moments and organizations. A piece that always fit exactly, so long as you looked carefully enough.

These are things I think of as I absentmindedly glance through Fabbi's book on Malatesta.

48

San Vicente puts a copy of *Anarchy* by Errico Malatesta
into his jacket pocket and breathes deeply. He cannot go to
the *Nuestra Palabra* editorial meeting because the police are
bound to be waiting for him when he gets there. Leave town?
Go to Librado Rivera's anarchist group in San Luis Potosí?
Or to Veracruz, where Fernando Oca from Santander was
now trying to take anarchist unions into the countryside?
Or to Bruschetta in Puebla? Or somewhere new, where the
CGT hasn't spread, like the mining districts in Chihuahua,
Coahuila or Zacatecas?

It is cold. He may have got hold of a suit, but he's still
short a shirt, and his pajama top will not go with the tie he's
carrying in his pocket. He likes this city, which is smoky
one day, and damp and rainy the next. He likes the neigh-
borhoods on the south side and the textile mills; he likes
the downtown cafés and walking along the Reforma in the
morning. But he does not like it enough to want to see it
from behind bars.

San Vicente makes plans. Settle a few accounts, leave a
few messages and make for the next town in a stolen car
before taking the train.

A boy comes up to sell him a newspaper. San Vicente

rummages around in his pockets, but ends up shaking his head. As the boy is moving off, he stops him by shouting, "Wait," and gives him the Malatesta book. It is best to travel light.

49

There's not much point in talking about it because nothing happened, although I did try to make it happen. It may be because we always lose, because our time hasn't come, because the best guys have all gone and it's just the jerks who are left—the useless bums who just make dreams and cannot turn them into lives. Maybe I didn't make the first train because of the business with the pistol, maybe I didn't catch Miño or the second train because of the mangos. Then I had to eat shit in Veracruz because of all that, and for eating shit in Veracruz I spent two days finding the jail, then I didn't go in because I didn't have the balls or I had too many plans, then because I didn't go in they took him away while I was out fucking, and because I was out fucking I only saw him from far away, so I couldn't tell whether he was smiling or not when they walked him up the gangplank. Maybe that was why.

I'm telling you all this so you'll know that well-meaning guys can be dummies, too, or more like, the better you mean, the bigger the dummy you are.

As I was walking home on June 13, 1923, I found Hilario waiting for me in the doorway. We'd both been fired from the streetcars, and were blacklisted, but I had a cousin working in the Balbuena railroad workshops, so I worked by the hour there under a false name—in electrical maintenance. Try as he could, Hilario couldn't find nothing and spent his time doing odd jobs for the union. As I saw him from faraway that day, I thought, "Damn me, Hilario, you're up to something, you're kinda worried," because he was shifting nervously from one foot to the other, and looking up and down the street while he waited for me.

"They got San Vicente—Pedro Sánchez," he said to me.

"How the hell...?"

"Twenty gendarmes with pistols burst into my place— no, more like thirty-five, and kicked him out of bed."

"Was he crashing at your pad?"

"Today he was."

"Shit," I said, because that was how it was with Hilario. He was a fighter and a good comrade, but one time I gave him a .38 to look after while I slept in the doorway at the Indianilla works during the strike, and he used it to mend his lousy socks with. I mean, with the pistol inside the sock and him darning away like a jerk.

"They'll kill him," Hilario said.

"No, not that, but they'll deport him up north. There they'll really fuck him over, there's a warrant out on him up there... Where'd they take him?"

"Beats me."

"You didn't follow him?"

"No, they worked me over," Hilario said. No kidding either. I hadn't noticed in all the rush, but he had one eye all closed up and bleeding under his brow from one hell of a pistol whipping.

I went into my place and began to look around in my trunk for my gun, taking no notice of my old man, the only one living with me in those days, since my old lady had taken off with the kids. I looked and looked, turning over books, papers, union minutes from the works and old shirts, but no gun. So I kept on saying, "Where are you? Where are you, you bitch?"

Finally, my old man kind of took pity on me, and said, "I hid her, son."

I turned round and there it was, my old .45, bigger than Kropotkin's history of the French Revolution—and with two full clips.

"You're one son-of-a-gun, old man."

"It's one hell of a business, son, and with you being a sleepwalker, likely as not you'd pick it up at night and shoot me."

"Come on, with what you eat I'd never kill you, even in my sleep," I told him. Then I gave him a message, as I knew what I was going to do. "Tell cuz I'll be back soon, to hang on to the job for me—I'm not going forever."

Then I ran out into the street, with the gun weighing down the jacket I'd slung over my shoulders, and Hilario following me.

"Where're we going?"

"To get another. One's not enough for what we're gonna do."

Hilario ran on with me all the way to comrade Mayorga's house—although he could see he was getting in deep. We knocked on the door, and no answer. Either he wasn't in, or he was fucking. He was famous for that. We hung around his house for three hours—a shack back of the Main Square in Jesús María Street—until he turns up bright and breezy.

"We've come for the gun."

"What now?"

"They got San Vicente, my son," I told him, although Mayorga's a good fifteen years older than me.

"And what are you going to do, comrade?"

"Shoot him out of there, so we need another gun."

"You going alone?"

"I'm going alone. This is personal, nothing to do with organizations. I'm going it alone."

Mayorga was real good about it. He went in and brought me his gun wrapped up in a copy of *Nuestra Palabra*. He didn't ask me when he'd get it back, or say anything.

Well, actually, he did say something. "If things don't work out, send a message with Hilario, to start up a big mobilization to make sure he doesn't get deported up North."

"Sure enough," was the last thing I said to him, and I left him in the dark because it was night by now.

The streetlamps were lighting up by the time Hilario and I got to Humboldt Street with our tongues all hanging out. A doorman stopped us, and I had to look at him real mean. We ran up the stairs into the newspaper offices.

Tomás Salas was sitting in front of his typewriter with his eyes closed. He was the crime correspondent and had helped the organization out a couple of times. They said unbelievable things about him, like how he wrote his copy blindfold and in one go. So we grabbed him right there, as it looked as if he was about to flip then and there.

"We need you, Tomás."

"Well, well. The men from the CGT, Bakunin's mob. What can I do for you?"

"They've arrested Sebastián San Vicente. Where would they have taken him?"

"San Vicente! But wasn't he deported on May 21?"

"He was here."

"Tell him he was called Pedro Sánchez," Hilario reminded me.

Tomás grabbed the phone and began to call his contacts, one by one, in the Mexico City Police Department, the Reserves, the Gendarmerie headquarters, Belén prison and Governor Gasca's secretaries. It seemed that San Vicente had vanished into thin air.

Suddenly, Tomás raised his head—which had been crouched over the phone whispering sweet nothings with the law—and said, "They've taken him to Veracruz."

"Mother-fucking Obregón." *

So I ran out to Buenavista railroad station which is where I lost Hilario—he had dozed off in an armchair in the newspaper building.

The train had left two hours before, and I cursed a lot. There were no friends around in the station. Then my mind started racing—I would rob a train and go to Veracruz at gun-point... And by the time I got to Puebla, there would be a hundred gendarmes waiting... I would break into the telegraph office and force them to send a telegram to stop

---

*(Translator's note): Alvaro Obregón. Mexican President at that time.

the train at the first station it came to, a telegram from President Obregón... And then what the fuck would I do? And then, chewing over stupid ideas, with one hand in each pocket on each gun—because in train stations they rob you if you're dumb enough, and if I was going to be unarmed as well as miss the train, then on my mother's grave I'd never live it down—I fell asleep.

I took the morning train to Veracruz, all cramped up because I'd slept in the station, and I dozed all the way to Puebla. There I sent a telegram to José Miño in Veracruz, asking him to pick me up when the train got in. I was going to need more help than Zapata in Chinameca* if I wanted to get San Vicente out in one piece.

So I went along, looking at the mountains and the plains, making all kinds of dumb-assed plans since I didn't even know what the jail was like, or what kind of security they had, or anything. Still, it doesn't hurt to make plans, or so I thought, so I made plans. And that's where the whole business went to hell in a handbasket because I was so busy making plans, that I didn't realize that the mangos I'd bought off an old lady were unripe, and after an hour and a half my guts were really playing up and I couldn't wait for the train to stop in Soledad del Diablo. I went straight to the bathroom there, and the train ride left me with a bad dose of the shits, just when I didn't need it. What screwed things up even worse was that there was no organization in Soledad

---

*Translator's note: Chinameca. The ranch where legendary revolutionary leader Emiliano Zapata was trapped and killed in 1919.

that I knew of—and I should know because I was the one that sent all the bundles of *Nuestra Palabra* all over the country, and there were no bundles for Soledad so I had to rob a milkman's horse and cart and gallop off to Veracruz. That wouldn't have been so bad, but the proletarian driving wouldn't understand my arguments even if I beat them into him, and I figure that with the rush, I didn't explain too well, and I had to reason the best I could with the horses, and force the driver along at gunpoint. Even then he wouldn't understand, and ran after me, insulting my dear mother, even though it wasn't her fault San Vicente had been taken in, or that the mangos on the train were unripe.

So I got into Veracruz very late, with two half-lame horses under temporary custody, and Miño wasn't anywhere to be found in the station. I thought the rest would be easy, that I just had to find the CGT local, see the comrades, find out where they were holding San Vicente, and get to work making plans, because, what the fuck, that's what I like most. But it wasn't going to be so easy. First, where the hell was I going to put the horses? You can't just leave them there, like they were a motorcycle, or something, without feeding them. If I just left them, who was going to feed them and get them back to the milkman in Soledad del Diablo? Because I had to give them back in running order. So I wasted three hours in Veracruz trying to find somebody or other who wouldn't fuck them or eat them. I mean, you can never tell, they've always had some really barbaric habits in ports, and not all of them were imposed by capitalism.

It must have been about nine at night when I got to the local. I was sweating like a pig and couldn't take my jacket off because my guns were flapping around, and besides there was nobody in the local, and I could hardly ask the cop on the corner because I was on a mission with fate, and cops don't understand fate, even if they do understand missions.

I slept on a park bench opposite the union local. I woke up when Miño shook me with more strength than good intentions. The sun was well up by now, damnit.

"'Salright, you know, I came back. HHHhhere I am, no hassles."

"What time didja get in, friend, and what's the big hurry?" Miño said. He was a Spanish anarchist, and too well dressed for my liking.

"San Vicente's in Veracruz. They've got him locked up, ready to deport him. We've got to find out where they're holding him, and which boat he's going on."

"Damn! When did they catch him? When did they bust him?"

"Well, I don't know if they fucked him up, they just took him in."

"You're such a smart arse. Where I come from, some one's busted when they're bloody well busted."

"It's the same here—when they fuck you up, you're fucked up.* They took San Vicente in the day before yesterday. And now he's here, in Veracruz."

---

*Translator's note: In this passage, Taibo is punning back and forth between Spanish-Spanish and Mexican-Spanish. In Spain, coger means simply to catch or grab. In Latin America, coger means to fornicate, or to fuck. The use of this verb leads to many embarrassing moments for natives of Spain traveling in Latin American countries—for instance, if they want to catch the bus.

"Let me see," Miño said, scratching his head. "As to when and how they're going to deport him, that's easy. As to where they're holding him, that too. We just ask our comrades from the prisoners' union."

"You're pretty damn advanced here if even the prisoners are unionized."

Miño didn't take much notice of me and went up the stairs in the union hall with me following on behind. But then, I suddenly remembered the horses...

"Wait a minute, I've got to see to the horses!" I shouted to the Spanish guy, who was beginning to get about as much as he could take of me.

The horses were fine, and Miño had found out a thing or two by the time I got back.

"He's going to be deported on the Alfonso XII, bound for La Coruña, right to my home town..."

"Shit, that's bad, if that's where they go around screwing the Christians..."

"San Vicente's an atheist so don't you worry about cursing him. The information's good. I spoke to Miranda from the seamen's union, and he tells me that that's how it is, that the Alfonso XII's the only thing that's outward bound right now, and the seamen were all talking about how someone dangerous is being deported although they didn't know about San Vicente. They thought he was a bank robber or some fancy con man because they get deported every day."

"So they're sending him back to Spain," I said to myself. "That's not too bad."

"Not too bad," Miño said, parrot-fashion.

"Where is he, then?"

"That's the hard part. I spoke to comrade Marín who went to sort things out with the prisoners' union, but there's no answer yet. Sit yourself down over there…better still, over here, and help me out with the newspaper accounts, which I've got to hand over to the assembly."

So that's how I spent the next few hours—in which I managed to take my jacket off, pistols and all, which I hung on an old clothes rack, which actually was the best piece of furniture in the office.

"Nothing, Miño, nothing," the woman said, coming into the room where the Spaniard and I were studying something called *The Mysteries of Non-Saleable Credit Sales in the Labor Union Press.* She was a fine-looking woman, well-stacked, just like I like them when I've got time for a bit of free-form wrestling with no referees—buxom, with a short skirt and garter belt on view which she only used to carry a razor with because it gets so hot in Veracruz, you've either got to be real fancy or plain stupid to use stockings.

"They ain't got him in the Degollado jail, he ain't down at police headquarters, Sánchez' men ain't got him in the military precinct, the Navy ain't got him, so he must have disappeared up his own asshole. Because he *is* in Veracruz—and you can tell that when you ask those officers and gendarmes from lieutenant up. That bunch of asshole-faggots have got him, all right."

"So where is he, comrade?" I ventured to ask.

"Who's this jerk?" she asked.

"You found me out," I said.

"Don't get like that with him, comrade Marín. He's the one who came down from Mexico City."

"Does he have a lot of balls?"

"Two, at least," I said so as not show off or anything.

"Whaddya wanna know for? You gonna get him out?"

"Can our comrade be trusted?" I asked Miño, just as she got real angry and turned as red as can be. Like I said, you've got to be careful with these Veracruz people because if they go around fucking horses who knows what they'll do to you.

"All right. Enough's enough. Both of you can be trusted— me too, at a push," Miño said, trying to bring some humor to bear which I hadn't seen from him the whole morning.

"Don't worry. I'll find out," the woman said, all smiles now, and went out as if the devil was at her heels.

"Just who's that, Miño? We never saw her in Mexico City."

"That's comrade Marín, married to Herón Proal. Mind how you go with her, brother, or she'll bite a couple of your fingers off, just like that."

And that's where the conversation ended. I spent the afternoon going over accounts. Then I went down to the first-floor assembly room and stuck my five-cents' worth in a bakers' union meeting, wrote an article on Ricardo Mella, went to see how my horses were doing. As night fell, there was fresh news.

"He's in Headquarters. Incommunicado. He's the only prisoner there, with a guard on watch and a machine gun post to the left of the gateway," comrade Marín said with a half-defiant smile.

"How many guards, apart from the one on watch and the one with the machine gun?"

"Two by the gateway, two or three more in an off-duty

room, apart from the ones I told you about. Night and day. You're going to have a real hard time of it, friend."

"Thank you for your best wishes."

"No. I'm not telling you because I like things that way. I'm telling you just the way it is."

"Will you take me there?"

"I'll get you close and show you. After that, you're on your own."

"That'll be your loss."

Two on the gate, high walls, another one on watch behind a window—comrade Marín had left that bit out. This was going to be a real mess. I walked around because the night air is real good for chewing plans over and because I liked walking around in the thick sea air by the port.

They charged me three pesos for minding the nags. If things went on this way, I'd have to rob a bank to get San Vicente back to Mexico City in one piece and to feed us both besides. I got into the driver's seat and my voice alone was enough for my horses to begin trotting around the sleepy Veracruz streets.

I stopped the cart ten paces away from the headquarters and climbed to the back where the milk bottles were. I needed a perfect plan, and I was going to have to spend hours and hours just thinking to come up with one.

"What are you doing here, sir? Are you planning to sleep here?" the soldier on guard duty asked me.

"Just until the morning since I have to make deliveries as soon as day breaks."

"So why don't you go to where they keep the other carts?"

"Well, because I was looking up the skirt of a lady in that place, they won't let me spend the night there."

"No? Well, just leave it here and I'll watch over it. After all, I'm on guard duty and it's no trouble. Just come and pick it up in the morning."

"Really, Sergeant? Would you really do me that favor?"

"Corporal Ramírez... But you'll have the milk ready for breakfast now, won't you?"

"Don't mention it." It seemed that the best plans in life needed no help from anybody.

I shook the reins and went through the gateway with my horses and the milk bottles tinkling behind me. It was true—there was a guardroom, a machine-gun post along the corridor and a lookout on the roof. Too many to get the artillery out and pick them all off at once.

"Ramírez, what the fuck's going on here?"

"The milk cart, Sergeant. We'll watch over it here, with your permission," the Corporal said out loud, and then went off to speak to the Sergeant, a guy with a wild-looking moustache and knife-fighter scars on him.

"On your way now, sir!" Ramírez shouted at me, and I went out onto the street.

The main door to the union hall was shut and all the lights were out, and I didn't know where to find Miño. I walked around town, cursing and swearing all the while. I ended up on the same park bench, under a leafy tree, with birdshit falling on me now and again, ready to sleep out in the open another night.

I was hassled awake yet again.

"All right now, I'm coming." It wasn't Miño this time,

but the ample Veracruz lady underneath the ample-boughed tree, looking at me with a more than indifferent ample smile.

"Don't you know there's a law against vagrancy in Veracruz and that you can't sleep on park benches?" she said.

"Comrade Marín, I need two sticks of dynamite," I answered.

You could see there were many roads leading to Rome with this lady—and a lot of friends making out they were Romans—because first she took me along to a fish monger's shop that was closed, then to a low-down cabaret where we drank some rum and danced some wonderful dances, then to see a blind man who played in a brothel doorway, then to her house, then to her bed, and then she got the dynamite out from under the mattress.

"But why didn't we do this in the first place?" I asked her.

"Because if I'd taken you straight to my house and my bed, you'd have thought I wasn't a lady."

It was a smallish room, not too big, with flowers—gardenias—on the bedside table, and two imposing pictures of Bakunin over the bed.

The gardenias—with their sweet, marvelous smell—took me away. I grabbed the dynamite with one hand, a breast with another, and turned out the light with another—so I guess I must have had three hands that night because that's how I remember things, just like I'm telling you now.

Well, that's how I remember things anyway, when I don't feel too guilty to mess it all up.

"Shit," said Miño, bursting the door open, "I just knew it."

I covered my balls and my wedding tackle up with a pillowcase, and looked for my gun with my other hand.

Three days running with surprise awakenings was getting to be a bit much.

"They're already taking him away. The boat's fuckin' well sailing today. Didn't you want to rescue him? They're deporting San Vicente today."

And so I ran and ran through the strects of Veracruz, with my shoelaces badly tied and my guns almost falling out of my pockets, out of breath on every damn corner.

And so I just saw Sebastián go up the gangplank and couldn't even tell if he was smiling or not.

Maybe it's because we always lose, because our time hasn't come yet. Or maybe I missed the train because I went around looking for the pistol, then I had to get off the train in Soledad del Diablo because I ate unripe mangos, then because I got off the train, I had to rob these two horses, and because I robbed the horses I...

50

"There'll be no coming back this time," San Vicente was thinking. "Now they're going to deport me to the United States or to Cuba."

This would mean changing his current prison for another one which without doubt would lack the virtue of a sea breeze blowing through the bars. "Another prison?" he wondered, trying to imagine it. "That'll be six now. Or is it seven?" And so he went over all the times he had been jailed, counting them on his fingers for lack of anything better to do. He was only counting formal imprisonment when he had spent a week or more inside, and not temporary lock-ups in military barracks or police stations. "Ideas cannot be jailed," he said to himself—and then added with an ear-to-ear smile, "but I can."

Mexico was over and done with, and so he went pacing round his six-by-six yard cell, touching the walls as he ruminated, cooking up a way to say good-bye, a farewell to a country where he had spent almost three years. "You can say good-bye to countries, but not to ideas," and he smiled again, savoring an almost personal joke, just made for monologues.

Would he have to account for those years or was it

enough to just let it go and hold onto those memories that would now be kept along with other memories, which in their turn were stored along with even older memories? Like where to put that chicken broth he ate at nightfall, or that cavalry charge that had been held back by weavers throwing stones in Tizapán. The sabers that glistened in the sun at daybreak and those unmoving faces, eyes staring at the horses' hooves, the crowd waiting for them, stones-in-hand. What was he to do with the mole that woman Elena had under her left breast which broke the woman's symmetry and drove him wild?

Where was he to put a nightmare that had woken him up in the middle of the night only to realize that it wasn't a nightmare and that the dream had run over into his sleeplessness? Where would he put that last cigarette he smoked with Phillips or the dull glow from the black Stetson that the seamstresses at the Palacio de Hierro had given him? How could he make quotes from Malatesta sound as musical as they did around a campfire, talking to the peasants from Acolman who seemed perfectly receptive to the Italian anarchist's thinking? There must be some place for all these memories—a notebook, a blank-paged book, a fish tank or a waistcoat pocket.

"A cardboard box to keep memories in," he said to himself as he kept pacing up and down the cell while he recited Segismundo's monologue out loud without thinking—something he had learned by chance when he was a child and did not want to forget: *HHHHere I am in a dream/ by such prisons sorely saddled/ and saw myself as I dreamed/ in some other charmèd realm/ What is life then, but turmoil?*

51

"Name?"

"Sebastián San Vicente Bermúdez."

"That your real one?"

"Quite so. First of all, all names are real if you use them properly... And what might yours be, Colonel?"

"That's besides the point. You are not interrogating me and neither do you have anywhere to write down any answers that I might give you."

"Here, in my head."

"Even so, what use is my name to you?"

"Nothing, just curiosity, I suppose."

"Age?"

"Twenty-seven."

"Place of birth."

"Gijón, Asturias, Spain. An iron-and-steel town, with fisheries and glassworks, on the northern coast of Spain, where coal from the Asturian mines is shipped out."

"I know. I think I saw it on a map once."

"And what did it look like?"

"I don't know... Like a dot, just like things do on a map. Marital status?"

"Single."

"Religion?"

"Are you serious?... None, of course."

"But aren't you an anarchist?"

"Of course."

"Isn't that a religion?"

"If you want to put it that way... Religion: Anarchist. It sounds funny. It has a ring to it."

"I'll put it that way. Length of your stay in Mexico?"

"Thirty months and five days."

"Did you enter the country legally?"

"The first time, yes. The second time, I walked across the Guatemalan border. And while I'm about it, I really should knock a month off the length of my stay in Mexico."

"Why did you enter the country illegally?"

"Because I do not believe in legality, and while we're about it, I don't believe in borders, either. There was no difference between Mexico and Guatemala. Just from one tree in the jungle to another. Trees don't recognize borders either."

"We can't deport trees."

"So much the better for them."

"And what were you doing in Mexico?"

"Just passing through."

"Just passing through?"

"Just passing through."

"On your way to where?"

"You tell me."

"Education?"

"The University of Life. I was taught to read and write by nuns. What I've read and written since then has all been my own responsibility."

"O.K. for me to put 'self-taught'?"

"Put what you like."

"Affiliated to any party or organization?"

"Yes, to the CGT in Mexico."

"And in other parts of the world?"

"That remains to be seen."

"What connection do you have with the Communist International?"

"None. Are we going to start with all that again?"

"With all what?"

"With the debate between the First and the Third International. I thought I was going to be done with that here."

"Don't worry. I don't give a rat's ass."

"Thank you."

"Do you have any charges pending trial in Spain?"

"No, none."

"In the USA or Cuba?"

"I suppose so, although I don't have any up-to-date information on Cuba."

"Doesn't matter... Did you take part in any illegal activity in Mexico?"

"According to whom?"

"According to me, my man. Don't make things difficult—according to Mexican law."

"I don't recognize..."

"Well, even if you don't recognize them."

"What do you want me to answer?"

"Just 'No.' I have instructions to deport you, not to detain or try you. The Mexican government just wants to get rid of you. We don't even want you in our jails. That's why

I won't ask if you fired on soldiers in the Uruguay Street shoot-out or not, nor what you had to do with the attack on CROM activists in Tlalpan, nor do I want to know if you held up the Guadalupana wages clerk in Atlixco. As you can see, I prefer you to be innocent."

"Well, if that's the way things are to be, I'll go over to the side of the angels... I don't suppose you're interested in knowing that four days ago, when I was detained in Mexico City, a Gendarmerie colonel and four soldiers beat me up for five hours. No, I don't suppose you're interested in that either."

"Do you have any money?"

"I suppose I could rustle up a couple of pesos."

"That's no good."

"For what?"

"For paying your fare."

"Oh well, not for that, no. If you're going to deport me, you'll have to pay."

"It seems that way."

"Yes it does, doesn't it?"

52

Well, it seems you really are going now, and I can't do much to stretch out this story that has been keeping us both company these last few nights. Nothing lasts forever, Sebastián, I tell you—not the typewriter either, which is now so used to my monologues that it doesn't even answer back. Your story has finished for me now in Mexico, but you will carry on with it beyond the Gulf Coast and the Veracruz palm trees. Where? I haven't got the faintest idea. All traces of you have been wiped out. The San Vicentes in the Gijón phone book don't know anything about you. There's no trace of you in the CNT archives in Amsterdam, nor any record of your participation in the Asturias revolution back in '34. Your name doesn't show up in the annals of the Spanish Republican Northern Army in the Salamanca archives. There's nothing on you in the French National Archives, and the FBI forgot about you after 1922, according to the U.S. National Archives in Washington. You are not where you ought to be. The newspaper section in the National Library Archives in Havana did not come up with your name when I asked them. Where the hell did you get to? Where did you take the Revolution? These are things that you should tell me. I sometimes think that you must have left some trace in some conversation or other, on a piece of paper or in a letter. Where did you get to? The Wobblies in Chile? The Chinese revolution from 1925 onwards? Hong Kong, Canton or Shanghai in 1927? Germany? Hamburg? Spain? Madrid, Barcelona or Andalucía? Africa? Some other palm trees? Argentina? I look through the 1925-28 collection of *La Protesta* in Valadés' archive. It is like looking for a wild goose on a moving map. Imagination might supply the missing links between the Sebastián San Vicente deported from Mexico in July 1923 and Otto Braun's (Li-teh's) Spanish friend on the Long March in China in 1934.

A bit of fiction might link the man gazing at the Gulf of Mexico with Romero's Spanish friend in the Huk rebellion in the Philippines. You might even say San Vicente was Sánchez, the Colombian, who helped Durruti to rob a bank in Buenos Aires. But the links cannot take the strain, they just crack up leaving a man standing on the wharf in Veracruz. A man who dissolves, vanishes into thin air in that thing which we—due to bad habits—call history, and condemn to the past.

From the wharf, seconds before you vanish, you give me a teasing smile. Tonight, from this typewriter, I smile back.

53

Twenty nautical miles off the coast of Veracruz, on board the Alfonso XII—a Spanish transatlantic liner—the man was freed from his handcuffs and taken out of the flag room. Since the Mexican government was paying the fare, he was granted a space in a second-class cabin along with two French citizens who had failed to find gold in the north of Mexico and were homeward bound, and with a Spanish storekeeper (Spanish family background, but born in Puebla) who was going to get married in his "home" town (Cebreros, Avila), to whom he did not yet know. The second mate, after settling him in and letting him out on deck—with none of the captain's snobbery—told him that the cuffs would be put on him again when the ship stopped in New York, after which he would be freed at the first Spanish port they put into—namely, La Coruña.

The second mate told him these things with some respect because rumors had been going around about the deportee these last few days to the effect that he was a dangerous anarchist. San Vicente listened in silence, as if concerned about other things, as if answering questions he had asked himself long since.

It was a remarkably clear day, and the coast could be

seen as a shadow on the horizon. And that is how he saw it—leaning on the banister, distracted only by a girl dressed in white who was playing with a cat.

He saw the coast, made out the palm trees, and the friends who stood stock still as the boat steamed away from them.

He could feel a fire burning inside. The fire of unrepeatable good-byes, the last good-byes, like *I'll never come back, we won't see each other again, ever.*

But these good-byes, these irrevocable good-byes, were a bit like saying *Be seeing you*, because when you lose something so intense it never quite goes away. It is captured forever, a bit like in the middle of a glass paperweight, an everlasting *Be seeing you*.

That is why Sebastián San Vicente allowed himself a tear for the American continent that was unwillingly slipping away from him.

54

July 1924

Circular: Land and Freedom Group
A. Bruschetta, Puebla.

   I am writing to notify all my
comrades of my change of address, which
from now on will be in the city of
Zacatecas, Hidalgo Street, # 125, Attic,
and to request you keep sending union
ideas and propaganda there just as you
have been doing here.

   I take this opportunity to request
that you send me news about Sebastián
San Vicente, a comrade who was with us
and whom you must remember. I have only
received a photo from La Coruña when he
disembarked there, and later on a post-
card from Bordeaux, France, where I
suppose he must be now.

Yours in anarchy,

A.B.

55

Interior Ministry
Political Affairs Department
Information Section
Press Analysis Section

REPORT 11908/2

We note the publication of an article
(enclosed) signed by Paco Ignacio Taibo
II in the "Unomásuno" cultural supplement
entitled "Sebastián San Vicente, a name
without a street," dated April 13, 1982,
about a Spanish anarchist of the direct
action tendency, active in Mexico between
1921 and 1923. This is the second article on anarchist violence published by
this author, who had written a previous
one in the same journal about a certain
Durruti, who robbed the La Carolina
offices in Mexico City in 1925 (ref. 11908/1).

For what it is worth.

(Handwritten note in pencil—"File"—and three illegible
letters forming a signature)

The illusive Paco Ignacio Taibo Dos (PIT II) was sighted in El Paso, Texas on December 9, 1999.